Counting on the Cowboy

Counting on the Cowboy

A Riverrun Ranch Romance

Karen Foley

TULE
PUBLISHING

Chapter One

FLAMES WERE ALREADY shooting through the roof of the abandoned warehouse on the outskirts of Last Stand when Jorie Russell arrived on the scene. Black smoke billowed over the tops of the nearby live oaks, and the acrid stench of burning metal filled the air. Despite the blisteringly hot summer in the Texas Hill Country, an intermittent breeze riffled the tall grasses in the nearby meadow and made the abundance of wildflowers appear as if they were dancing.

The town's firetrucks and water pumpers were already on site, but, thankfully, the dozen or so firefighters who had arrived with them were too busy pulling hoses, shouting orders, and manhandling equipment to notice her. Police Chief Highwater hadn't yet arrived, either, which boded well for her. He'd have already cordoned off the entire area and set up a perimeter, preventing her from gaining access to the property. She had only minutes before he and his officers did show up, so she needed to act quickly.

She pulled her little SUV into the farthest corner of the gravel, weed-choked parking lot, well away from the emergency vehicles. She'd been on her way home from a long day's work at Honeyman's Veterinary Hospital when the firetrucks raced up behind her, sirens wailing and lights flashing. She pulled over and allowed them to pass, and then followed them. She'd been horrified to see flames engulfing one side of the old warehouse that had once been a distribution center for local peaches. All she could think about was the feral cat who lived in inside amongst the wooden pallets and old peach crates. The last time she'd checked on the animal, the cat had been in the advanced stages of pregnancy. Had she delivered her kittens? Were they even now trapped in the warehouse, too frightened or disoriented to escape?

Keeping a wary eye on the firefighters, Jorie turned off her engine and slipped out of the driver's seat. She opened the back of the SUV and retrieved a small pet carrier and a can of cat food with a pull-tab lid. The town of Last Stand had a trap-neuter-release program for the feral cats in the region, and Jorie always carried several small animal crates in the back of her vehicle, as well as food and first aid supplies. She'd been trying to capture this particular cat for weeks, but the sly feline was proving to be elusive. With one eye on the first responders, she walked as quickly as she could along the side of the building toward the back of the warehouse, where she knew she'd find an unlocked door. She'd accessed the warehouse numerous times before, but promised herself if there was any sign of smoke or flames, she would abandon her mission. But she had to at least try to rescue the scruffy calico she'd affectionately dubbed Taco.

As soon as she was out of sight of the firefighters, Jorie broke into a run but when she rounded the back of the building, she was dismayed to see the access door that had always hung askew, had been secured with a thick padlock. There were no windows and no other doors that she could see. If Taco was inside, she would have no way to escape! Jorie turned to run back to the front of the warehouse . . . and barreled directly into a man's hard, unrelenting body.

She gave a startled cry and would have lost her balance, but a strong hand reached out to steady her. Jorie looked up into the face of a firefighter wearing a heavy yellow turnout jacket and helmet. But this wasn't just any firefighter, and Jorie's heart nearly burst with joy as she recognized Luke Claiborne, her first and only crush from the time she'd been thirteen years old. Not that he had a clue. She'd heard he'd gotten out of the army and had recently returned home. In that first instant, she had a swift impression of the changes the past years had wrought.

He was bigger.

Harder.

And he still had the ability to make her go a little spongey in the knees. She would have thrown her arms around him in relief, but he held her firmly away and for the first time, she noticed the expression on his handsome face.

Luke Claiborne was furious. *With her.*

All the times she'd daydreamed about meeting him again, she'd never imagined this particular scenario. Worse, there wasn't so much as a flicker of recognition in his eyes, although she did notice he wasn't at all shy about giving her the once over. He raked her with a look so thorough that Jorie felt momentarily exposed.

"What the hell are you doing?" His voice was harsh with disbelief, even as his dark eyes flickered between the cage and the can of food she carried, to the padlocked door. He knew exactly what she'd hoped to do, and Jorie could see the knowledge seriously pissed him off.

She found herself floundering for words, still reeling in disbelief that Luke Claiborne was standing in front of her, in the flesh. The fact that he didn't seem to recognize her shouldn't have piqued her so much. After all, the last time he'd seen her, she'd still been a gangly teenager. But she hadn't been prepared to feel as if she was still fourteen years old in his eyes, not when she'd hoped to show him she was a woman now.

"There's no fire in this part of the warehouse," she said lamely.

"Doesn't matter. The situation could change in a heart-beat. Do you have even the slightest instinct for self-preservation? Do you?"

Jorie could only stare mutely at him, wide-eyed with em-barrassment that he'd caught her doing something so foolish. She'd heard he was working cattle on his family ranch. When had he traded his cowboy hat for a firefighter's helmet?

"That's what I thought," he snapped, when she didn't answer. "This is an active fire scene, and you have no business being here. Get back in your car and go home."

He still had one gloved hand wrapped around her arm, and now he began to haul her away from the building. But Jorie dug her heels in and resisted him.

"No, wait! There's something I need to do!"

Luke stopped and stared at her, his expression incredulous. "Are you fucking kidding me? If you don't get your pretty little ass moving, I *will* throw you over my shoulder and carry you back to your car. Then I'll have Chief Highwater arrest you for trespassing. Do you understand?"

"Please," she said. "I wouldn't have gone in, except I'm desperate! There's a cat that lives inside, and—"

To her astonishment, Luke pushed his face close to hers, until a scant inch of space separated their noses. She should have been alarmed, but all she could think was that his eyes weren't actually black, as she'd always believed. They were a lovely shade of coffee brown and she could even see specks of gold in those dark irises, like Spanish coins tossed into a wishing well.

"Lady," he growled, interrupting her, "I don't give a shit if the Queen of Sheba lives here. In case it's escaped you, this entire building is going up in flames. Even if you were able to find a way in, you'd be overcome by smoke and *you would die* before you ever found the damned cat which, by the way, is probably long gone. Cats have more sense than some people do, apparently."

"She has kittens. *Please.*" Jorie could feel tears threatening and hated that she had so little control over her emotions. But the thought of Taco perishing in a fire was almost more than she could bear. She'd dedicated her life to saving animals and each time she lost one, it was like losing a beloved friend. "*Please.*"

To Luke's horror, the woman's beautiful hazel eyes welled up with tears. He had two younger sisters so he got exactly how this worked. But even knowing he was being played, he felt his resolve slip a notch.

"Jesus H. Christ," he muttered, and half spun away, tempted to make good on his threat and carry her bodily to her car. He couldn't believe she'd been willing to put her own life at risk for a damned cat. When he'd spotted her making a break for the back of the warehouse, he'd bolted after her, suspecting the worst. But now, seeing the genuine distress in her lovely eyes, he found he couldn't dredge up the will to refuse her. He actually understood how she felt.

"Okay," he finally bit out as he turned back toward her. "I'll look for the cat, but you are leaving. *Now.*"

Her expression cleared, and she gave him a smile so brilliant that, for a moment, Luke felt a little dazzled.

"Thank you!" She held out the crate to him.

"Yeah, yeah," he muttered, ignoring the crate. "Let's get you the hell out of here and then we'll worry about the damned cat."

She kept pace beside him as he strode toward the parking lot, talking hurriedly as if she was afraid he might change his mind. "That door wasn't padlocked the last time I came by. I've been inside there a dozen times. I don't know who locked it."

"Probably the owner, tired of people trespassing on his property." He gave her a meaningful look.

"She lives in the middle section of the warehouse where all the pallets and old peach crates are stacked," she continued, ignoring his remark. "She's a multi-colored cat, mostly black, but with orange and white patches. I call her Taco. If she's in there, you can coax her out with the tuna and then locate the kittens. If there are kittens, that is."

"Wait." Luke stopped beside her car. "You mean to tell me you don't know for sure if the cat is actually in there? Or if there are any kittens?"

She at least had the grace to look embarrassed. "Last Stand has a trap-neuter-release program, where we try to catch feral cats and neuter or spay them before returning them to the environment. I've been trying to bring this cat in for weeks now, but she's pretty cagey. She was definitely pregnant the last time I saw her, but I'm not sure if she's had them yet, to be honest. I checked on her a few days ago and she looked ready to drop them any time."

Luke gave a short laugh. "Oh, man, this just gets better and better. You're going to send me into a warehouse fire, where you think a feral cat *might* be living beneath a pile of fucking kindling, and where there *might* be kittens. But you're not sure. But hey, no problem. I'll try not to get burned alive during your damned scavenger hunt."

He wouldn't admit—even to himself—that he'd be willing to walk barefoot over hot coals to earn another smile from her. She was, hands down, the prettiest woman he'd seen in a long time, and her pale pink hospital scrubs couldn't disguise the sweet curve of her backside or the elegant slenderness of her shape. There was something familiar about her that he couldn't quite put his finger on, but it would come to him. Hers wasn't a face he'd easily forget.

"Do you have to swear so much?" she asked, but her tone lacked any true censure.

No, he didn't, but since he no longer wore a uniform, he figured he no longer had to follow the protocol he'd lived by as a military police officer. As a civilian, swearing was his new prerogative. And maybe, if he kept up the bad-ass attitude, she wouldn't realize she'd found his weakness. He was a sucker for a pretty smile.

Now she held out the crate to him. "This is your job, right? It's what you get paid to do."

Luke snorted, but took the crate. "I'm part of the volunteer fire department, honey. I don't get paid for any of it." He indicated the car. "Just get the f—just go. Please."

He waited while she climbed into the driver's seat and started the engine. Before she put the vehicle into gear, she looked at him and worry creased her smooth brow.

"Be careful, okay?"

"*Now* you worry," Luke muttered, and watched as she drove out of the parking lot and was directed around the emergency vehicles. Past the hydrant, where three fat water lines were now connected, she pulled her car over to the shoulder of the road. Satisfied that she wasn't going to pull any more harebrained stunts, Luke made his way back to the tanker trunk for his breathing apparatus.

"What's going on?" Fire Chief Harding asked, as Luke pulled a protective hood over his head and shrugged into an oxygen pack.

"Lady over there says a mother cat and kittens are living

in the warehouse. I told her I'd go in after them." He pulled on his gloves and adjusted the face mask on the hood where the oxygen hose would connect, before securing his fire helmet.

Chief Harding frowned. "Does she have any clue where in the warehouse they are?"

"Right in the fucking middle, where else?"

"Okay, I'll give you ten minutes. They're knocking the flames back on the far side, but it's an old structure and any support beams could be compromised. Take Jenkins with you."

Luke nodded as Chief Harding gestured for Pete Jenkins, one of the senior firefighters in Last Stand, to join them. After hearing what Luke intended to do, he quickly donned his own breathing apparatus, but not quickly enough. Luke groaned inwardly when he saw his brother Evan jogging toward them.

"What's going on?" Evan asked, sweeping his gaze over Luke. "Why are you suited up? You're supposed to be manning the tanker."

"Yeah, well, now I'm not," Luke replied. "I'm going in after a mother cat and her kittens."

"You're kidding me, right?" Evan gestured toward the warehouse. "That roof could collapse any minute. The cat's probably not even in there."

"I have it on good authority that she is," Luke fibbed.

"We should go in now, before the fire spreads to that part of the structure," Pete advised.

"I'll go with him," Evan said. "They can use you here,

Pete."

"You don't have to go with me," Luke protested, torn between annoyance and amusement over his brother's overly protective stance. "I'm a big boy."

"We're wasting time." Evan grabbed his own breathing apparatus and quickly suited up. "Let's go."

Luke bristled but didn't argue. Granted, he was new to the department, having joined the Last Stand firefighters just six weeks ago, but he'd completed the training and he knew what he was doing. But his twin brother had always taken the lead on whatever they did. Just eight minutes older than himself, Evan had done the same their entire lives. But Luke knew Evan's high-handedness today had nothing to do with their birth order and everything to do with wanting to ensure Luke's safety. No matter how many times Luke assured his brother that he had recovered from his combat injuries and was *fine*, Evan treated him with kid gloves.

Luke knew he meant well, but Evan's protectiveness rankled. A year had passed since an improvised explosive device, or IED, had ended his career with the 503rd Military Police Battalion. Physically, he felt fine, but the doctors had refused to clear him for combat duty, so he'd gotten out. He could have taken a desk job, but no way was he cut out for that shit. He needed to be boots on the ground, making a difference. He just wished his canine partner, Elsa, had been able to get out of the military with him, but she'd been reassigned and had redeployed before he'd been released from the hospital.

Luke couldn't think of the German shepherd without his

chest tightening. He'd been her first handler and together they'd saved countless lives in both Iraq and Afghanistan. Not a single soldier had died under Elsa's watch, because her instincts had been that good. He hadn't had a chance to thank her for her loyal service or even say good-bye. While he was profoundly grateful she had survived the explosion without injury, he hated thinking of her with a new handler, establishing the same kind of tight bond that he had shared with her during their five years together.

"We'll keep you wet," Chief Harding said now, bringing Luke back to the present. "Just watch your heads."

They entered the warehouse through the door at the back of the building, using a bolt cutter to break the padlock. Inside, they switched on their headlamps. The smoke was blinding and their flashlights actually made the poor visibility even worse, like high beams in a fog. Angling the beam downward, Luke took careful note of their surroundings. They were in a corridor littered with debris. Luke used his pike to feel his way along until they came to an open area. Smoke billowed in from a nearby wall where paint was blistering and the wood had an eerie red glow. As the woman had indicated, the space was filled with wooden pallets and crates.

Feeling a tap on his shoulder, he looked up to see Evan.

"This place is a fire trap!" Evan shouted, and used his hatchet to point overhead, where flames licked along several ancient beams and plumes of black smoke oozed from the wood. Above the beams, the metal, corrugated roof had holes in it, but not enough to allow the deluge of water from the tanker truck to penetrate the interior of the building.

Even as Evan said the words, the beam made an ominous cracking noise, and a shower of sparks and flaming debris rained down onto the warehouse floor, threatening to ignite the wooden pallets and crates. On the far side of the space came a loud groaning sound of metal, and one side of the roof gave way, collapsing into the interior with a tremendous crash, smashing crates and pallets and sending plumes of thick dust and smoke into the already-polluted air. Water gushed into the opening as the firefighters turned their hoses onto the opening. Evan's radio crackled and Captain Harding's disembodied voice carried clearly.

"Claiborne, report! You boys okay? Over!"

"Roger that, Captain, we're good, over!" Evan replied.

"That roof isn't going to hold," Captain Harding advised. "I need you out of there, now! Over."

"Affirmative. Over and out." Evan turned to Luke. "There's no way we're going to find anything in this," he shouted. "We have to go!"

But Luke was on his hands and knees, searching beneath a pile of overturned crates. A beam of light from his head gear had picked up the reflection of two glowing eyes in the darkness beneath the rubble, and now he pulled off his glove and shoved his arm beneath the pile of wood, searching cautiously.

He felt Evan grab the back of his turnout coat and give a hard tug. Glancing over his shoulder, his brother's face was hard with frustration. "We have to go!"

"I found them!" he shouted, and carefully drew forth a

tiny, mewling kitten whose eyes hadn't yet opened. Luke guessed it to be no more than a day or so old. He handed the little creature to Evan, who tucked the kitten into a pocket of his turnout coat, and then retrieved three more kittens, handing each one to Evan. Only then did the mother cat finally appear, looking frightened and stressed, and panting hard. "That's it," Luke crooned softly. "Come here, kitty."

When it seemed she would retreat back beneath the fallen pallets, Luke snatched her by the scruff of the neck and rose to his feet, holding the growling cat protectively within the curve of his body.

Evan clapped a hand on his shoulder, steering him back the way they had entered. "Let's get out of here before this thing decides to come down on our heads."

He had to shout to be heard over the thundering of water on the metal roof. As they passed beneath the overhead beam, it groaned loudly and sent another shower of sparks down on top of them. But then they were outside and moving away from the structure, and Evan was carefully withdrawing two of the kittens from his jacket pocket to cradle them in his gloved hands.

"Didn't you hear me in there?" Evan demanded, when they were safely away from the building. "I was shouting to you. You can't just ignore me because I'm your brother, Luke."

"I wasn't ignoring you. I had my hands on the kittens," Luke said, avoiding Evan's eyes. "I couldn't just leave them."

Evan stopped and stared at him in disbelief. "You're not wearing your hearing aid, are you? Jesus, Luke. You'll put yourself and the rest of us at risk because of your damned pride."

Luke frowned. "There's too much ambient noise. I do better without it."

"Uh-huh." Evan began walking away, but turned so that Luke could see his face—so he could read his lips. "Keep telling yourself that."

Blowing out a hard breath, Luke caught up with his brother. Evan was right, but Luke hated wearing the damned earpiece. It was a constant reminder of everything he'd lost, and the hearing in his left ear was the least of those things.

"How're the kittens?" he asked, changing the subject.

"Little buggers wouldn't have had a chance," Evan observed, turning his attention to the tiny kittens in his hands. "Speaking of which, let's get momma cat some oxygen. She looks like she's struggling."

They rounded the warehouse and were walking toward the firetrucks when there was a deafening crack, as if thunder had erupted behind them, followed immediately by a booming crash. Both Luke and Evan turned to see the entire roof of the warehouse collapse inward, sending a plume of flames and black smoke into the air. They exchanged a meaningful look.

"Five more minutes, and that would have been us under that rubble," Evan said, his voice grim.

"But it wasn't." Luke lifted the mother cat to a more comfortable position in his arms. She was panting heavily and beneath his hand, he could feel the rapid beat of her heart. "Let's get her some oxygen."

As they approached the trucks, the woman in the SUV jogged over, still holding the pet carrier. "Oh, thank goodness!" she gasped, seeing the cat. "I can't believe you were able to find her!"

"Yeah, I'm fine, thanks for asking," Luke said.

Her hazel eyes flew to his, and maybe it was the heat of the day, but he could have sworn her cheeks turned pink. "I'm glad you're okay. Do you want me to take her?"

"Why don't you take these little guys first?" Evan extended one kitten toward her. "We'll administer some oxygen to momma cat, make sure she's okay."

"Thank you, Evan," she said, and carefully transferred the first kitten to the pet crate.

Luke looked sharply at his brother, but Evan was fishing in his jacket for the remaining kittens.

"You two know each other?" A single thought hammered through his head: *Please don't let them be involved.*

"Uh, yeah, it's a small town," Evan muttered.

"I'm a vet tech," the woman interjected, as if that said it all. "Let me take a look at her."

"Her breathing is labored and her heart rate is accelerated," Luke said, and put out a gloved hand to keep her back. "Let us do this first, and then you can take her."

"Here are the other kittens," Evan said, and handed her the remaining two.

Despite their plaintive mewling, the mother cat barely responded to the sound of her babies. Her eyes had closed to mere slits and she panted rapidly. The woman took the kittens and placed them carefully inside the pet carrier, which had been lined with a soft, fleece blanket.

"The kittens seem healthy," she observed. "No obvious trauma or signs of oxygen deprivation. They can't be more than a day old. Will Taco be okay?"

"A little oxygen will help her rally." Evan pulled a portable oxygen tank from the back of the truck and deftly fitted a plastic tube attached to a face mask. Luke held the cat securely as Evan tested the oxygen flow and then fitted the mask over the cat's face.

"So you're a tech vet, huh?" Luke asked, as they hunkered over the cat. "Do you work at the clinic here in Last Stand?"

"I do, yes. I'm Jorie Russell, by the way."

Luke glanced at her, but her attention remained fixed on the cat. "I'm Luke Claiborne, and this is my brother Evan. But I guess you already knew that."

She lifted her hazel gaze to his. "Yes, I know who you are," she murmured.

"So, how do you and Evan know each other?" he asked again.

He didn't miss the swift look that passed between them, and his heart sank. The bro-code pretty much guaranteed that if Evan had ever dated this woman, then she was off-limits to Luke. He would never disrespect either of his brothers that way.

"It's been a long time," Evan said, glancing at Jorie. "How're you doing, anyway?"

"Fine," she said brightly. "Great, actually."

"You seem familiar," Luke mused. "Have we met before?"

Jorie shrugged. Reaching out, she gently stroked Taco's fur. Luke noticed her hands were slender, the fingers long and delicate and devoid of any wedding or engagement rings.

"I'm a friend of your sister's," she said. "I used to hang out with Emma when we were just kids, whenever she visited from New York. I did a lot of sleepovers at Riverrun Ranch, but that was a long time ago, so I wouldn't expect you to remember."

Relief rushed through Luke.

She hadn't been involved with his brother.

She was his sister's childhood friend, which was why she'd seemed familiar to him. Luke's younger half-sister, Emmaline, had lived in New York with her mother for almost her entire life, but had recently moved back to Last Stand. Growing up, she'd spent every school vacation at the ranch, and she'd been friendly with a couple of the local girls.

Luke had a distant memory of a skinny girl with a long, flaxen braid that had swung to her waist. He hadn't paid much attention to any of Emmaline's friends since they were so much younger than himself, but he did recall Jorie had liked to hang around the barns and paddocks and watch as he and his brothers trained new horses. As she fixed her attention on the cat, Luke studied her. She'd changed over the past ten years or so.

A lot.

He never would have guessed that leggy young girl would grow up to be such a knockout. Her white-blond hair had darkened to an ash blond, but some lighter streaks lingered, ribboning through the long tendrils. She was still slender, but in a way he knew other women probably envied.

Taco began to squirm in his arms and Evan removed the oxygen mask. "That did the trick. She seems to be perking up nicely. Give her plenty of water, and I think she'll do okay."

"I think you're right," Jorie said, and gently lifted the cat out of Luke's hands. "There, now, you're okay," she crooned, stroking the cat's fur. "Come say hello to your babies."

Luke watched as she placed the cat inside the pet carrier with the kittens. Taco nosed each of them, before settling down in a corner to wash her offspring as they crawled closer to her.

"So what will you do now?" he asked. "Bring them to the clinic?"

"I'll keep them at my place until the kittens are old enough to be adopted, and then find them good homes." She pushed a single finger through the wire of the crate and gently stroked Taco's fur. "But I think I'll keep this one."

"Okay, good luck with that," Evan said and rose to his feet, clearly anxious to do something more exciting now that the cat had been rescued. "C'mon, bro, we still have a fire to put out." He dismantled the oxygen mask and coiled the plastic tubing, before he stowed the gear back into the truck.

Jorie picked up the pet carrier and looked at Luke. "Thank you for what you did. Both of you."

"You're welcome," Luke said. "But no more running into

burning buildings, agreed?"

"Not unless I have to," she demurred.

Luke bent forward so that his face was level with hers. "Not ever. Understood? This is no fucking joke."

"Hey, bro," Evan said, putting a hand on his shoulder and pushing him back. "Easy. She meant well."

Luke shrugged his brother's hand off, but didn't break eye contact with Jorie. "I'm serious."

"Okay, I won't go into any burning buildings," Jorie said, but a hint of a smile lurked in one corner of her mouth, as if his vehemence amused her. "I promise."

Luke watched as she walked back to her car with the pet carrier in her arms. Removing his helmet and protective hood, he scrubbed a hand through his hair. "Damn fool woman."

Evan laughed. "Yeah, I can see she completely repulses you."

Luke shot him a glower, and then shoved his helmet back on. "I hope I never run into her again."

"Uh-huh, sure." Evan grinned, and then turned and walked toward the warehouse.

"At least not under these circumstances," he added, but Evan was already out of earshot.

Chapter Two

"LUKE CLAIBORNE HAS changed," Jorie grumbled, stirring cream and sugar into her coffee. "I can't believe I ever thought he was 'all that.'"

"I remember a time when you claimed he had magical DNA, irresistible to all females." Across the small café table at Last Stand's local coffee shop, Java Time, her friend, Jessie Montero, hid a smile behind her coffee mug. "But he did rescue your cat and her kittens. So he can't be all bad."

A week had passed since the warehouse fire, but her encounter with Luke Claiborne was never far from Jorie's mind. She'd spent years mooning over him as a teenager, building him up in her mind as some kind of romantic hero, when the reality was far different. She recalled again what it had been like to have all that testosterone directed at her. His language had been appalling, but hadn't really shocked Jorie. She'd heard worse from her own grandmother. No, what had bothered her the most was that even when he'd been furious, she'd found him incredibly sexy. In spite of his cursing and threatening to bodily remove her from the scene, she'd felt *safe*. What did that say about her, or her taste in men? Maybe her grandmother had been right. Maybe she *was* no better than her mother, who had always preferred bad boys.

Jorie couldn't think about her mother without feeling sad and angry. Where was she now? Was she even alive? Her grandmother's funeral, nearly ten years ago, was the last time Jorie had seen Lily Russell. And she suspected the only reason her mother had even made an appearance was to find out if she'd been left an inheritance. But Jorie's grandmother hadn't owned anything of value, unless you counted the rundown mobile home and ten acres of land it sat on. She'd left both to Jorie. Her mother had been furious, and hadn't even stayed for the reception. The guy she'd brought with her—and there was always a guy—had driven her away in an old Cadillac that belched black smoke as it pulled out from the cemetery.

"Well, there was no magic to be seen, just pure arrogance," Jorie declared. "Let's just say he was a reluctant hero, and not at all shy about letting me know what he thought about my plan to save Taco and her babies." She paused. "You probably know him best. Has he always been so . . .?"

"Abrasive?" Jessie offered helpfully.

"Exactly."

"Let's just say the military changed him. He was never exactly lighthearted, but I actually believe he feels things more than most people. If he's like the guys I know, he's probably not comfortable with that, so he deliberately comes across as tougher and meaner than he really is. Don't let it fool you."

"Ha. He's not tough; he's just a jerk."

But instead of agreeing with her, Jessie tipped her head

and considered Jorie thoughtfully. "My grandmother has always had a soft spot for Luke, and she doesn't put up with bullies or jerks. So I have to believe there's more to him than what he shows to the world."

Jessie's grandmother, Rosa-Maria Montero, was both the housekeeper and cook to the Claiborne family, having worked at Riverrun Ranch since the Claiborne brothers were little boys. She'd been like a surrogate mother to all the Claiborne children, lending warmth and stability to the male-dominated household.

"How do you know so much about him?" Jorie asked, curious. "That seems pretty insightful for someone who hardly ever sees the guy."

Jessie shrugged. "Sometimes I help my grandmother when she's working at Riverrun and I notice things, that's all."

Jorie hesitated. "So you're not, you know, hung up on him yourself?"

"What?" Jessie's eyes rounded, and she gave a bark of surprised laughter. "No! Trust me, he's not the brother I'm interested in."

"Wait." Jorie leaned across the table, unable to keep the astonishment out of her voice. "You're interested in Luke's brother?"

"So what if I am?"

"Which one? Evan?"

Jessie made a dismissive sound. "No way. He's too much of a player for me, and unlike Luke, he hardly takes anything seriously."

Jorie sat back in her chair and stared at her friend in disbelief. "You like *Holt*?"

"Why do you say it like that?" Jessie demanded, frowning.

"He's a little old for you, don't you think?"

"No. He's thirty-four. I'm almost twenty-six."

The oldest of the Claiborne clan, Holt was also the most intimidating of the three brothers, in Jorie's opinion. Of course, Luke could be intimidating, too, but with Holt, it was different. Where Luke was all bold energy and bad language, Holt was cool and reserved. He'd been married once, but it had ended badly and he had returned to Riverrun Ranch to help his father run the cattle operation. He had been a full-grown man when Jorie and Jessie had still been in high school.

"Hmm." Jorie made a non-committal sound and took a sip of her coffee. "I just remember him being so . . . *serious*. I'd be terrified to even flirt with him."

"But you'd flirt with Luke?" Jessie asked slyly.

Thinking of Luke caused a bright bolt of awareness to shoot through Jorie. She'd had a thing for him since she was thirteen years old and had become friends with Emma. Whenever she'd been invited to Riverrun Ranch, she'd lived in hopeful anticipation of seeing Luke. Unlike his brothers, he had coal-dark hair and his eyes had seemed as black as a pirate's. His brooding intensity had both frightened and fascinated her. As a teen, she'd spent endless hours down by the barn, hanging on the fence rails and watching him work cattle or helping to train a new horse. Nobody looked better in boots and Wranglers than Luke Claiborne. Whenever he'd see her, he'd touch the brim of his hat and give her a curt nod, which had made her feel very grown up and special. That he'd noticed her at all had both thrilled and amazed her, considering he was four years older than she was. Most boys his age would never have looked twice at a girl that much younger. She'd known then that Luke hadn't been like most boys. Then he had enlisted in the army and the next time she had seen him, he hadn't been a boy any longer.

"Luke doesn't seem like the flirting type," she finally said, remembering his threat to bodily remove her from the warehouse fire. "He's more like the throw-you-over-his-shoulder-and-carry-you-off type."

Jessie laughed. "You say that like it's a bad thing."

Jorie felt her face turn warm beneath her friend's knowing look. She'd been serious. As much as Luke aroused unfamiliar feelings in her, he also unnerved her a bit with his brusque manner and rude language. She forced herself to smile over the rim of her mug. "Maybe that's why I've always kept my weight down. Makes it easier to carry me."

Jessie gave a burst of surprised laughter, and soon Jorie found herself laughing too. She loved their Saturday morning ritual, when they could both escape their routines and meet at Java Time for coffee and girl-talk. They had been friends since middle school and there were no secrets between them except, apparently, that Jessie had a thing for Holt Claiborne.

"Uh-oh, don't look now but the object of your affection just walked in," Jessie murmured, her eyes riveted on the door behind Jorie.

But Jorie's senses were already on high-alert, having heard the deep baritone of Luke's voice as soon as the door of the café had opened. She wished she had worn something nicer. She wished she had applied some makeup. She wished she was anywhere but here, certain her emotions were written on her face for anyone to see. And then it was too late.

"Hey, Jessie, how're you?"

Jorie looked up to see Luke and Evan standing at the side of their table, their cowboy hats pushed back on their heads. Evan gave her a conspiratorial wink, but there was an intensity about Luke that made Jorie want to squirm. Right now, she felt dwarfed by his height, and vulnerable beneath his shuttered scrutiny of her.

"Hi, guys," Jessie smiled. "Nice to see you both. Do you remember Jorie Russell? We used to spend time at the ranch with Emmaline, whenever she was home."

Luke's eyes still rested on her and Jorie had to force herself to sit still and not fidget beneath his stare. "Yeah, I sure do remember Jorie," Luke replied. "We, uh, ran into each other at a warehouse fire last week. How's the cat?"

"Taco? She's fine. And so are the kittens. Thank you for asking."

"Been staying out of trouble?" he asked, and his dark eyes gleamed with amusement. "No trespassing or breaking any laws since I last saw you?"

"Don't tease her, Luke," Jessie said. "She's not used to your humor."

"Woman needs a handler," he murmured as his eyes lingered on her. "Someone to keep her safe since she has zero instincts for self-preservation."

Jorie found her heart rate accelerating beneath his scrutiny, but couldn't prevent a subtle examination of her own. He wore a pair of faded Wranglers and a dark-gray Henley jersey with the sleeves pushed up over his forearms. The soft fabric hugged his chest muscles and emphasized the breadth of his shoulders. He had his thumbs hooked casually into the front pockets of his jeans, and Jorie couldn't help but notice how big and capable his hands looked. They were the strong hands of a man accustomed to hard work, but she'd seen how gently they had handled the kittens. She couldn't help wondering if he'd touch a woman with the same tenderness?

"Jorie? Earth to Jorie!"

With a start, Jorie snapped her attention to her friend. "I'm sorry, what did you say?"

Jessie looked at her with a mixture of exasperation and amusement. "Evan asked if you were still living out by Hickory Creek."

Jorie couldn't prevent her gaze from flicking to Luke's, and she saw the barest hint of a smile lurking in the corner of his mouth. He *knew* he distracted her. Worse, he enjoyed it.

She tipped her chin up and shifted her attention to Evan. "Yes, I'm living in my grandmother's old place. She passed shortly after I graduated high school and left the property to me."

There was a momentary silence and Jorie could almost read their thoughts. Why would anyone *want* that property?

Located on a scrubby piece of land on the far side of Hickory Creek, her grandmother's house was actually a double-wide mobile home that had seen better days. The ten acres of land surrounding the mobile home had grown wild for decades, and Jorie had given up trying to tame it.

Jorie's grandmother had raised her from the time she was eight years old, after her own mother had abandoned her. Her childhood hadn't been an easy one, but her grandmother had done the best she could for her. After she died, Jorie had started a wildlife rehabilitation center in part of the mobile home. She'd always had an affinity for animals, and actually preferred their company to most humans. In the beginning, she had only handled small animals that had been brought into the veterinary hospital. Because the hospital only treated domestic animals, the squirrels, cottontails, and other small wildlife brought in by well-meaning residents would otherwise have been euthanized. So Jorie had brought them home with her, and had turned her kitchen into a triage and recovery center. But as word had spread, people had begun bringing her other wildlife they found—raccoons, beavers, and even a baby deer.

The only part of her grandmother's property that she maintained was directly behind the trailer, where she kept enclosures for the various animals she rescued and rehabilitated. She knew the place looked run-down and neglected, but she consoled herself with the knowledge that nobody could even see the trailer from the road. Besides, she had made a conscious decision to put whatever money she earned into the care and treatment of the animals she looked after.

Maybe someday she'd sell the land and buy something nicer, but for now, it served its purpose.

Luke frowned. "You live out there by yourself?"

"I do."

"That's pretty remote."

Jorie shrugged and smiled. "I don't mind."

"You could probably sell it," he continued. "Get yourself a place closer to town."

Jorie felt herself bristling at his tone. Clearly, he didn't think very much of where she lived. That shouldn't have surprised her, since the land beyond Hickory Creek was Last Stand's equivalent to the wrong side of the tracks. She knew some people in town looked down on those residents who lived out on Hickory Creek Road, but she hadn't expected that kind of judgment from Luke.

"Really," she said, keeping her tone mild, "I'm fine, and it suits my purpose. I don't mind that it's remote. I actually prefer the company of my animals to most people."

She didn't mean for Luke to take her words personally, but could tell from his frown that he had.

"So," Jessie said, her tone bright as she blatantly steered the conversation to safer ground. "We're here just about every Saturday morning, but this is the first time I've seen you boys here. What's up?"

"We had an early call this morning," Evan said. "Gas leak over by the elementary school, but everything's fine now. We're on our way home, but decided to stop in and grab a coffee first."

"You really don't get paid for what you do?" Jorie asked,

looking at Luke.

"Nope."

"Then why do you do it?" she asked, curious.

"Why do you rescue your fu—your cats?" Luke countered, retracting the F-bomb before it fully dropped. "Nobody's paying you to do that, right?"

"That's different," Jorie countered. "Somebody has to do it, and I don't see anyone else lining up to volunteer."

"My point exactly," Luke said smoothly. "Someone has to do it. Evan and I just happened to answer the call."

"Ha." Jessie leaned back in her chair and smiled at Luke. "Don't pretend you do it out of the goodness of your heart. I think I know you both better. You'd go stir crazy if you weren't doing something that gets your adrenaline pumping. Am I right?"

To Jorie's amazement, a grin spread over Luke's face, transforming it.

He had a dimple.

Jorie hadn't known that about him, and she felt her silly, girlish crush come rushing back. She felt a little starstruck. Thankfully, that infectious grin was directed at Jessie and not her; otherwise, she was sure he would have noticed how flustered she'd suddenly become.

"You might be right," he was saying.

"I know I'm right," Jessie said, her tone smug. "You Claiborne men are all the same."

"Well, I'm not sure the same can be said about Holt," Evan mused. "He's pretty risk-adverse. He prefers to bury himself in accounting ledgers, and his biggest thrill is attending the annual cattlemen's convention. In fact, the closest he's come to a meaningful relationship is deciding which cow he's going to breed with which bull."

Now it was Jessie's turn to look a little flustered. "I'm sure that's not true," she said. "He's just . . . responsible."

"The man's a damned paragon of virtue," Luke said, but his tone was mild and lacked any real condemnation. "I mean, when's the last time he even had a date?"

"Okay, can we please talk about something else?" Jorie asked, sliding a wary look at the nearby patrons. "Nobody wants to hear this."

"You're blushing," Luke murmured, looking at her with renewed interest.

"No," she protested, knowing she was. "I'm just unwilling to talk about your brother's private life in a public coffee shop!"

"But that's just it," Luke said. "Holt has no private life."

Jorie glanced at her watch. "Oh, will you look at the time?" she exclaimed. "I have to get going."

No way was she going to sit here and talk about sex, even if it was only implied. She'd never been good at hiding her thoughts, and she absolutely did not want Luke Claiborne to guess how she felt about *him*. She still liked him.

A lot.

She just didn't know if she could trust him. He'd changed since he was a teenager, and she found herself a little overwhelmed by his brash masculinity. She didn't spend a lot of time in the company of handsome, single men and Luke Claiborne made her nervous. She hadn't been kidding when she said she preferred the company of animals to most humans, and without any animals around to ground her, she had no idea how to act. She was sure he found her both unsophisticated and uninteresting.

She glanced at Jessie, who was staring at her with a mixture of confusion and surprise. "I thought you said you had the day off!"

Pushing her chair back, Jorie stood up. "I do but I, um, I promised to go in and administer some meds. Thanks for the coffee, Jess. I'll give you a call later this week."

Without looking at either of the Claiborne brothers, she mumbled a good-bye and made a beeline for the door. She needed to escape, because she was afraid Luke saw too much. And if she stuck around much longer, he might figure out how she felt about him. And that was the last thing she wanted.

Chapter Three

J ORIE'S ESCAPE WAS foiled when she was forced to pause at the door to allow a group of teenagers to enter.

"Did you forget something?"

The deep voice spoke directly into her ear and caused her to jump. Luke stood just behind her, so close that she could feel his body heat. Jorie wanted to coil herself around him like a small garter snake and absorb his warmth. Instead, she stared stupidly at him.

"What?"

"You forgot your purse." He held up one hand and she saw her small pocketbook dangling from the end of his finger.

Jorie smiled, before reaching out and taking the handbag from him. "Thank you."

Embarrassed, she turned to leave but Luke was there ahead of her, opening the door and holding it for her. Wordlessly, she stepped onto the sidewalk and began walking toward the spot where she'd parked her car, surprised when Luke fell into step beside her.

"You okay?" he asked. "I didn't say something to offend you, did I?"

"Like my needing a handler?" She made a scoffing noise. "No, that's not at all offensive!"

Luke gave her an unapologetic grin. "I'm available for the job, in case you're looking. I have all the required training, and can even provide references."

Jorie's body went warm all over. Just the thought of Luke Claiborne handling *her* was enough to send her heart rate into overdrive.

"Thanks," she said drily. "I'll keep that in mind. I actually have to go to the clinic, like I said," she fibbed. "Weren't you getting coffee with your brother?"

"Nah, I've already had my quota of caffeine for the day." A hint of dimple appeared in one lean cheek. "Evan tells me I need to be nicer to people, so I'm cutting back."

Jorie felt a smile tug her mouth. "Something tells me you could go cold turkey and it wouldn't improve your temperament."

Luke grinned, and the dimple made a full-Monty appearance. "You're probably right."

They had reached her car, and Jorie stopped walking long enough to fish through her pocketbook and retrieve her keys. "This is me," she said, indicating the small SUV. "Thanks again for what you did for Taco."

"Sure, no problem." He made no move to leave, just stood on the sidewalk with his thumbs hitched in his pockets, watching her.

"Well, then, have a good day," she said, and unlocked the driver's door.

Luke lifted a hand and waited until she was behind the

wheel and had closed the door before he turned away. Jorie sat and watched him for a moment, admiring his lean frame and broad shoulders. With a groan, she pulled herself together, and thrust the key into the ignition, surprised when the engine cranked over but refused to start.

"No, no, no," she muttered, and turned the key again, with the same results. She pumped the gas as she turned the key, but still the engine refused to turn over. Worse, Luke had paused on the sidewalk, and now he was walking back toward her car. "Damn."

Luke opened her door and leaned down, bracing one arm on the top of the frame. He pushed his hat back on his head and grinned at her. "Having problems?"

Jorie gave him a helpless look. "It's never done this before."

"The engine is turning over, so it's not the starter. Could be the fuel pump, or maybe a bad fuse."

"Great." Jorie blew out a hard breath, and then retrieved her phone from her purse. The last thing she needed was for her car to be out of commission. Last Stand didn't have a taxi service, and she wasn't exactly within walking distance of town or the veterinary clinic. Worse, she didn't have the cash reserves to pay for an expensive car repair, which meant she'd have to put it on a credit card that was nearly maxed out. "I'll call for a tow."

"Do you mind if I try?" Luke asked.

Jorie shrugged. "Sure."

Gathering her purse, she stepped out of the car. Luke straightened enough for her to slide past him but even so, she was acutely aware of him. As she ducked under his arm, she caught a whiff of leather and spice and something that was uniquely him. The combination was heady. She watched as he folded himself into the driver's seat and slid the seat back to accommodate his longer legs. He experimentally turned the key, but the engine refused to start. After a moment, he looked at her.

"I'm no expert, but I think your fuel pump is gone. I'll have it towed to a friend's garage; he'll get it done quickly and give you a fair price."

Jorie waited as he climbed out of the car. "Thank you, I'd appreciate that."

"Let me give you a ride to the clinic. I can wait while you do your thing, and give you a lift home afterward."

"Oh, no, that's not necessary," she protested, realizing she was about to be caught in her own lie. "I don't want to put you out. Jessie's still in the café, so I'll just have her bring me over."

Luke shook his head. "She's already gone. I watched her leave about two minutes ago."

"Seriously?" Jorie peered down the street toward the coffee shop, willing her friend to appear. She really, really didn't want to accept a ride from Luke, but it would be a long, hot walk back to her house. Reluctantly, she turned toward him. "Okay, if the offer still stands, I accept. But I don't need to go to the clinic; if you could just drop me off at home, that'd be great."

To his credit, he didn't ask why her plans had suddenly changed, but the glint in his dark eyes said he knew she'd fibbed about needing to go to the clinic. "My truck is parked down the road. Grab what you need, and I'll call the garage to have them come get the car."

"What about Evan? Won't he be expecting you to drive him home?"

"Evan has his own vehicle," he replied.

"Right." Jorie kept several spare pet carriers in the back of her car, along with some basic medical supplies and food items that she used to entice animals into the crates. She put the medical supplies and food into a tote bag, and closed the rear hatch. "I guess that's it."

"I'm going to leave your car key under the driver's floor mat," Luke said. He worked the key free from her key ring and handed the remaining keys to her. "Your car will be fine, and I'll make sure Matt gets out here quick."

Jorie wasn't worried. She couldn't imagine anyone would be interested in stealing her pet carriers. She had enough trouble finding people who wanted to adopt a pet. "Thanks again. I appreciate you giving me a lift."

Luke glanced upward at the cloudless sky. "Yeah, well, today's going to be a scorcher. Hate to see you try to walk home once the temps hit one hundred, and they will."

Jorie followed him down the sidewalk, trying not to feel deflated by the knowledge he was only helping her out of a sense of duty. The firefighter in him had an obligation to protect the public, and that was the only reason he wasn't leaving her stranded in town.

They reached a dark-green pickup truck. Luke came around to the passenger side and opened the door. Jorie set her tote bag on the seat and pulled herself into the truck as Luke closed the door and came around to the driver's side. She looked around the cab with interest. There was an official-looking handheld radio in the center console, along with a stainless-steel travel mug and a pair of sunglasses. A small, framed picture was attached to the dash, and she leaned closer to peer at it. Wearing full combat gear, Luke squatted next to a German shepherd. The dog wore a flak vest, and there was no mistaking the adoration in the animal's eyes as she looked up at Luke. Jorie knew Luke had been a military police officer, but she hadn't known he'd worked with a military dog. She found the knowledge reassuring; anyone who worked day in and day out with animals had to be good at their core. She'd sensed that about Luke, but this drove it home for her.

But as Luke settled himself in the driver's seat, Jorie inched closer to her door. She couldn't help herself. In the confines of the cab, he seemed bigger and more masculine than he had in the coffee shop. She had to remind herself that this was Luke, whose family had been nothing but kind to her since she was eight years old and Emmaline had decided she and Jorie would be best friends. He slid the sunglasses on and, after cranking up the air-conditioning, eased the big truck onto the main road. Jorie studied him covertly as he drove in the direction of her house.

He had slashing black brows and a clean, square jaw, and it seemed every part of him was layered in smooth muscle. Even his thighs beneath the worn denim looked muscular. Until last week, Jorie hadn't seen Luke Claiborne in nearly five years, and then, only from a distance. He'd joined the army right out of high school and had spent much of the next twelve years deployed to one dangerous hot spot or another. Through Rosa-Maria and Jessie, she knew he'd been a military police officer. He'd been home a couple of times in the ensuing years, but she'd only actually seen him two or three times, and never this close.

He'd changed.

He'd always kept to himself, but the army had hardened him. Or maybe she'd just never really known him to begin with.

"Something on your mind?" he drawled.

"What?" Jorie started guiltily.

"You've been watching me like I'm the big, bad wolf and you're Red Riding Hood." He slid her one swift glance, inscrutable behind his sunglasses. "Wondering if I'm going to eat you?"

Jorie gaped at him, her imagination running riot by the soft suggestion in his words. Or had she only imagined it? "Of course not," she finally managed to say. "Anyway, I wouldn't be much of a meal."

She felt his swift scrutiny like a palpable touch, and goose bumps of awareness raised on her arms. "You *are* a little on the slender side. A tasty snack, then."

Jorie gave a brief, humorless smile. "Right."

A snack. Something to be devoured quickly and then forgotten.

They had driven out of town and a small bridge took them over Hickory Creek, which all but a dried-up streambed this time of year. Then they were traveling down a remote road with woods and fields on either side. Up ahead, Jorie indicated a mailbox on the side of the dusty road.

"You can drop me off here."

"I'll take you up the driveway," Luke said.

"No, please just drop me here." The last thing Jorie wanted was for Luke to see the double-wide trailer she called home. He'd been raised at Riverrun Ranch, with a housekeeper and all the amenities his wealthy father could provide. She didn't want to see his revulsion. More than that, she didn't want to see his pity when he realized how meagerly she lived.

As a girl, Jorie had been in awe of both the Claibornes' ranch house and their lifestyle. She'd done sleepovers with Emmaline, and she still remembered what it had been like to have breakfast served on the back patio, within sight of the Pedernales River and all those beautiful acres of Claiborne land. They'd had three dogs who slept on Emmaline's bed each night, and her father hadn't even seemed to mind. Mr. Claiborne had been kind to Jorie. In retrospect, Jorie guessed he knew about her family situation and felt bad for her. She'd been the poor girl from the wrong side of town, whose floozy mother had gotten pregnant and run off with a wrangler. Only neither parent had been interested in raising her themselves, so she'd ended up on her grandmother's doorstep. How many times had Rosa-Maria sent her home with a bag of Emmaline's clothes, insisting Emmaline had outgrown them? At the time, it hadn't occurred to Jorie that maybe those clothes could have been passed on to Emmaline's younger sister, Callie. She had accepted them gratefully, knowing her grandmother could never afford anything as nice for her and wouldn't choose to spend money on quality clothing for Jorie, even if she'd had it.

Now Luke pulled the truck over to the side of the road, and thrust it into park. Turning in his seat, he removed his sunglasses and looked at Jorie. "Give me your number and I'll call you when your car is ready."

"Why don't you give me the name of the garage and I'll call them directly?" Jorie countered. She'd learned early on not to depend on other people when she needed something done. Better to look after herself.

A smile tilted one corner of Luke's mouth, and his expression was quizzical. "Afraid I'm going to put you on speed dial and harass you? Call you in the middle of the night?"

Jorie shrugged. "It's been known to happen."

"To you? Is that why you carry that around?" He indicated the small pink canister of pepper spray she carried.

Unbidden and unwelcome, a memory resurfaced. Years had passed since the incident with Mason Childress, a local boy whose father had made his millions in the oil shale fracking industry. She hadn't actually thought of Mason—or the violent attack that had occurred in the cab of his pickup truck—in many months, but realized that was exactly why she no longer gave out her phone number, or anything else, for that matter.

"Let's just say a girl can never be too careful," she replied, and opened her door. "Thanks again for the ride."

"Jorie." Luke leaned over the seat, his gaze direct and intense. "If someone fucked with you, give me his name. I promise you, he won't do it again."

Oh, man, this guy was way too perceptive. Jorie would need to be careful around him. She forced herself to give him a reassuring smile. "No need. It was a long time ago."

Even then, Luke seemed reluctant to let it go. Jorie stood there, looking at him expectantly, until he muttered a curse beneath his breath and straightened in his seat. "Call McGuire's Garage, ask for Matt."

"Thank you."

Jorie started to close the door, but Luke leaned over and put a hand on the handle. "If you need a ride anywhere, give Jessie a call. If she can't help you, have her call me. Rosa-Maria has my number; I'll come get you. Got it?"

Jorie nodded, too surprised by his unexpected offer to say anything. She watched as he turned the truck around and drove away, the big tires stirring up dust on the road. With a sigh, Jorie hitched her tote bag over her shoulder and made her way down the long, dirt driveway. Eventually, the overgrown trees and underbrush opened onto a meadow, where tall grasses and wildflowers grew in abandon. A half dozen beehives stood at one edge of the field, easily accessed by a path that Jorie kept mowed.

In the middle of the field stood the double-wide trailer she had called home since she was eight years old. A wooden handicap ramp led to the front door, built during her grandmother's final years when she had been confined to a wheelchair. The exterior of the mobile home showed its age, with faded paint and numerous rust stains from where the windows had once leaked. Jorie had repaired the worst of the problems and spent precious money remodeling the kitchen. For now at least, the structure was watertight. But when she tried to view the house through a stranger's eyes, she saw only a rundown trailer in an overgrown field, out in the middle of nowhere.

Behind the trailer, near a line of trees, she could just see the large, outdoor enclosures where she kept the raccoons, foxes, and other wildlife that were in the process of being rehabilitated for release back into the wild. She hadn't planned to become a wildlife rehabber; it just sort of happened. For as long as she could remember, she'd brought home abandoned or injured wildlife in the hopes of saving them. Her grandmother had been furious, certain she would contract rabies or worse, and had forbidden her from bringing any animals onto her property. But Jorie had learned to be sneaky about it, hiding them in the old tool shed behind the house. In those early days, she'd lost as many as she'd saved, mostly because she'd lacked resources and she hadn't had a clue what she was doing.

When she turned eighteen, her grandmother had died, leaving her the trailer and the property, and she'd redoubled her rescue efforts, converting part of the mobile home into a triage center for the wildlife she rescued. She'd obtained a job as a receptionist at the local veterinary clinic, where she'd observed and learned as much as she could. Two years later, she'd been shocked when Dr. Honeyman offered to help her get into a vet tech program at a local college, offering her a tuition loan. The two-year program had changed her life and provided her the skills she needed to start her own wildlife rehab operation.

She had never been avaricious. Life had taught her that she needed very little. Right now, she had twenty-six helpless creatures depending on her for their very survival. How many times had she told herself that as long as she had the means to care for them, that was enough? She'd never wanted anything more. Her experience with Mason had made her wary of men, and she'd never allowed herself to dream about a relationship where she was an equal, where her thoughts and opinions mattered.

But as she climbed the ramp to the front door, a thread of unease untangled itself in her chest. She'd wanted Luke Claiborne for as long as she could remember, the way a child might want a coveted treat they saw in a shop window, but couldn't afford. He'd been nothing more than a girlish wish. Until now, she'd never had any reason to hope their paths might cross, or that he would ever see her as a desirable woman—if he even noticed her at all. But the way he had looked at her today caused all her youthful yearnings to resurface.

Suddenly, Jorie wanted *more*.

She wanted Luke Claiborne in every way a woman could want a man, and the realization scared her to death.

Chapter Four

LUKE WATCHED AS Matt McGuire hitched Jorie's car to his tow truck. He and Matt had been friends since grade school, although they hadn't seen much of each other in the dozen or so years since they'd graduated high school.

"Listen," he said now, as Matt finished securing the coupling. "Give me a call when you're done with the repairs. I'll pay for whatever's wrong."

Matt pushed back the brim of his baseball cap. Overhead, the sun was relentless and sweat trickled down the side of his face and darkened his shirt in patches. "Sure. Probably just the fuel pump, like you said. Shouldn't be too much."

"I don't give a fuck about the cost," Luke said, knowing it was the truth. He had plenty of money set aside, but he'd stake his life on the fact that Jorie had little or nothing to spare. "In fact, do a tune-up and check the fluids while you're under the hood. Make sure it's road-worthy."

"Jorie ain't going to like that." Matt mopped his face with a rag. "She's funny that way. She's proud."

"Screw her pride," Luke replied. "Her pride isn't going to be worth shit if that car breaks down and leaves her stranded somewhere."

Matt nodded. "Okay, but you should let me give her an invoice, even if it's just for twenty bucks. Then she won't feel beholden to you. Beholden women tend to feel resentful and embarrassed, and then they avoid you. That what you want?"

Luke didn't know what he wanted. Maybe to stop thinking about Jorie Russell altogether. Yeah, that would be a good start. But as soon as he thought about not thinking about her, he remembered how she'd blushed at his reference to Holt not getting any. He shouldn't have found her embarrassment so freaking appealing. He'd seen some of the worst of humankind during his deployments and now here was this girl who was like some fucking Snow White, and he couldn't get enough.

He'd been out of the army for too long. He'd gone soft. But the thought of Jorie distancing herself from him, of maybe even *avoiding* him, was definitely not what he wanted.

He blew out a hard breath. "Nah, I don't want that. Go ahead and bill her for something small. Tell her it was a spark plug or something. But keep it under fifty bucks and tell her the towing is free. Add it to my bill."

"You got it."

"And call me first, okay?"

"I heard you the first time," Matt assured him. "You two seeing each other or something?"

Or something.

Luke didn't know how to describe what was going on with him and Jorie Russell, only that she'd taken up way too much real estate in his brain this past week. He'd felt a rush of pleasure when he'd spotted her sitting with Jessie at the coffee shop, and hadn't resisted the urge to go over and say hello, even knowing his brother would torture him for it later.

Now he shrugged. "She's a friend of Emmaline's. Wouldn't be right not to help her out."

"Uh-huh." Matt's tone said clearly he wasn't buying it.

Luke scratched the bridge of his nose and shifted his weight. "Hey, you grew up out by Hickory Creek, didn't you?"

"Yep. Not too far down the road from the Russell place."

"So, did you know Jorie when we were kids?"

"I knew who she was, but we didn't hang out or anything, if that's what you're asking."

"So, what was the deal with her? I remember something about her mother abandoning her?"

"Yeah, something like that. I don't know the details, but I think she got dumped at her grandmother's place after her mother took off somewhere. No idea what happened to her father, or if he was ever in the picture."

Something screwed tight in Luke's chest, and he drew in a long, slow breath. He told himself he wouldn't feel sympathy for Jorie just because her mother had abandoned her. His own mother had walked out on him and his twin when they'd been little more than toddlers, and they'd turned out fine. Of course, they'd had Rosa-Maria, who had been as constant as the North Star. She may have been their housekeeper and cook, but honestly, Luke considered her to be more of a maternal figure than his own mother, whom he rarely saw now that he was an adult. These days, she was living out on the West Coast with her third husband.

Whatever.

"What was Jorie's grandmother like?"

Matt laughed. "Well, she sure wasn't into baking cookies. I remember one time she ran my daddy off her property at the end of a shotgun. Ornery old lady, that's what I recall."

"No shit," Luke said. "Why'd she do that?"

"One of our dogs got into her yard. Apparently, she didn't much like animals. If my dad hadn't gotten there so fast, she'd have shot the dog, sure as rain. My kid sister still harbors a grudge over that incident, even though it happened over a decade ago."

"I didn't know you had a younger sister," Luke said.

"Yeah, she's nineteen." Matt shrugged. "Typical teenager, all moody and shit. I just steer clear."

Pulling out his wallet, Luke peeled off several twenty-dollar bills and handed them to his friend to cover the towing cost. "Thanks, man. I appreciate you taking care of this."

"Yeah, no problem."

Luke watched as Matt maneuvered the tow truck onto Main Street and drove away, the little SUV in tow. As he climbed into his truck and returned to Riverrun Ranch, he couldn't stop thinking about what Matt had told him. No wonder Jorie had found her calling in rescuing animals in need. She was like an abandoned kitten herself.

As he drove through the gates of Riverrun Ranch and caught sight of the main house, he felt something shift and loosen in his chest. This was home. He'd always loved the ranch, but he'd never given much thought to how fortunate he was. Some of his best memories were of riding out before dawn with his father and brothers to work the herds. He'd always loved being a cowboy, but for as long as he could remember, he'd wanted to join the military. There had been something about the camaraderie and potential danger that had appealed to him. Jessie Montero had been right in that respect—he liked getting his adrenaline pumping. If his father had wanted something different for him, he'd never let on. He'd given Luke his blessing, and had even driven him to the recruiting station to enlist.

Luke had spent twelve years with the army and found his true calling with the 503rd Military Police Battalion. Not only was the 503rd the only MP unit to be airborne, but it also had a K9 unit. After basic training and combat training, Luke had graduated first in his class from the military police course and had gone on to become a K9 handler. Elsa, a German shepherd, had been just sixteen months old when they'd begun training together, and their bond had been instant and unbreakable. Hell, they'd even jumped out of a helicopter together, with her strapped tandem-style to his harness. Where he went, his dog went. Where his dog went, he went.

At least, that had been the case until the day of the explosion, when he'd had to make a split decision to follow Elsa or rescue a toddler from the middle of the street. He had missed Elsa's signal, and was lucky they hadn't both been killed when the IED she'd sniffed out had exploded mere yards from where they'd stood. Three months later, following the doctor's assessment that his hearing loss was profound and permanent, he'd made the decision to get out of the army. If he couldn't work with Elsa, he just didn't see the point. He would never again be a military working dog handler. If he couldn't hear commands, or distinguish sounds, he put himself, his dog, and the unit he was protecting in jeopardy. He'd only been home for six months and while he still wasn't sure what he wanted to do with the rest of his life, he had time to figure it out because he had substantial savings and a family who supported him, no matter what.

What did Jorie Russell have? From what Matt had said he knew about her, precious little.

Luke parked the truck and climbed out, intending to go into the house and grab a shower when he saw movement down by the barns. His oldest brother, Holt, and Emmaline's fiancé, Cort Channing, had recently started their own bull breeding business, and one of the barns had been designated for that purpose. Seeing his father and Holt disappear into the barn, Luke changed direction and headed toward them.

Inside the barn, the air was warm and pungent with the smell of fresh hay and manure. Swallows flew high in the overhead rafters, and an orange barn cat dozed sleepily in a patch of morning sunlight. A dozen cows had been secured in holding pens and were either contentedly chewing the sweet hay, or lowing softly. He spotted Holt and his father in the office, bent over a computer screen. He knocked lightly on the door.

"Am I interrupting?" he asked, as they both looked up.

"Nah, we're just reviewing the lineage of the cows, trying to decide which one we should breed with Audacious," Holt said, straightening.

Audacious, one of the finest bucking bulls in history, had been dead for more than twenty years, but his semen had been frozen for future use. A bull bred from his stock would command damned good money.

Remembering Evan's assessment of Holt's love life, Luke had to suppress a grin. Tall and lean, with the same startling blue eyes as his father, there was no question Holt was a good-looking guy. He could probably have any woman he wanted, but he'd been hurt one too many times. Luke didn't have to be a shrink to know that losing your mother *and* two stepmothers before you were twelve years old could result in commitment issues. But Holt's failed marriage had been the final straw. After his divorce, he'd returned to Riverrun and had thrown himself into running the ranch with a single-minded intensity. Ten years had passed since the divorce but, as far as Luke knew, his brother hadn't been involved with anyone. That, or he'd been very discreet.

"What's on your mind, son?" Gus asked. In his early sixties, his father had a shock of silver hair and vivid blue eyes in a warm, tanned face. He wasn't a tall man, but he exuded an air of command and, when he looked at you, he gave you his full and undivided attention, as if nothing else was as interesting to him as what you had to say at that moment.

About to ask what his father remembered about Jorie Russell's family, Luke suddenly realized how his older brother would interpret his question. His father would give him reliable information, but Holt would assume he was interested—romantically interested—in Jorie. If Holt thought for even a second that Luke might have a soft spot for a woman like Jorie, he'd never hear the end of it. Holt might not have a love life to speak of, but he'd be ruthless in tormenting Luke if he thought Luke might have anything resembling a tender bone in his body. He probably thought Luke was a player, like Evan. The truth was, Luke probably led an even more monastic existence than Holt did.

"Nothing," he fibbed, and leaned against the doorjamb. "Just thought I'd come down and see what you were up to. Do you need any help?"

Holt cast an amused glance at him. "Thanks, but we're good."

"Glad to hear it, because I was just being polite," Luke said, grinning. He'd be the first to jump in if a horse needed breaking, cattle needed moving, or equipment needed fixing. But he drew the line at bovine genetics or handling an insemination gun.

He watched idly as they pulled up the statistics of several cows, and after listening to them debate the pros and cons of each, grew restless and wandered back outside. Breeding bucking bulls held little interest for him. He'd prefer to be in the saddle, herding cattle or riding fences. He could think clearly when he was outdoors, surrounded by the beautiful Texas Hill Country. He walked over to the nearby paddock and folded his arms over the top rail of the fence and watched a mare with a new foal, enjoying the warmth of the sun on his face and the sound of the cicadas in the trees.

"Okay, son, what's on your mind?"

Luke turned to see his father coming out of the barn, and together they began walking back toward the main house. Two of the ranch dogs, Rip and Sam, trotted happily at their heels, tongues lolling. Reaching down, Luke gave Sam a fond pat.

"Do you remember a girl named Jorie Russell, one of Emmaline's friends?"

"Sure I do. Pretty little thing, but half-starved in my opinion. I hear she works over at the vet clinic now."

"Yeah, that's right."

"And you want to know about her." Gus never broke his stride.

Luke shrugged. "I'm just curious. Her car broke down in town this morning and I gave her a lift home. Did you know she lives out on Hickory Creek Road?"

"Sure, I know. Her momma was a wild one, or maybe she was just looking for a way out. She ran off with some wrangler right out of high school. Came back a few years later with a child in tow, but her daddy refused to take her back."

"But they raised Jorie?"

"No, not as I recall. At least, not right away. Jorie's grandfather was a mean son of a bitch, and he sent his daughter and her baby packing. The way I understand it, Jorie spent years being shuffled between relatives who either didn't want her or couldn't keep her, for whatever reason. It wasn't until after her grandfather passed that her grandma agreed to take her in. She was probably eight or nine years old by then. That's when she became friends with Emmaline."

"What happened to her momma?"

Gus shrugged. "No idea, but probably nothing good. All I know is she left that child with Helen Russell and took off again. You might ask Rosa-Maria. There's not much that happens in Last Stand that she doesn't know about."

They had reached the house, and now they climbed the steps to the big, wraparound porch. Gus eased himself into a chair, and Luke sat down beside him. Rip flopped at his feet and Luke reached down to absently stroke the dog's ears. From their vantage point on the porch, they could see the Pedernales River that flowed lazily past the back of the property, and the rolling hills where cattle grazed beneath stands of live oaks. Beyond the barns and outbuildings, Luke could just see the roof of the ranch manager's cabin. Evan held that position now, but he preferred to live in the main house where he had easy access to Rosa-Maria's cooking.

At his father's urging, Luke had taken the small cabin for himself.

"What's your interest in Jorie Russell?" Gus asked, smiling as Rosa-Maria appeared with two tall glasses of cold lemonade. "Thank you, Rosa-Maria."

"My pleasure, *señor*. Is there anything else I can bring you?"

"No, but maybe you can help Luke. He's interested in Jorie Russell. Do you remember her?"

"Dad," Luke protested softly, feeling like an idiot. "I'm

not *interested* in her, I'm just curious."

"Of course I remember Jorie," Rosa-Maria said. "She's a friend of my granddaughter, Jessie. She's a sweet girl."

"What happened to her mother, do you know?" Gus pressed.

"No, *señor*. I believe she has been gone for many years. Jorie lived with her grandmother, but that woman never did right by her. The poor child didn't have many clothes and was half-starved. I remember sending her home with some clothes that Emmaline had outgrown. I would try to fatten Jorie up while she was here, but she never ate much. Is there anything else, *señor*?"

"No, thank you, Rosa-Maria."

"Why didn't anyone report it?" Luke asked, when Rosa-Maria had returned to the house. The Last Stand Police Department took a dim view on child abandonment and abuse. In fact, he couldn't imagine anyone in Last Stand ignoring a child in need.

"There's no crime against being poor," Gus said drily. "And you can't force a child to eat if they're not hungry."

"I'm not sure I know what that's like," Luke said, wryly. "I think I was always hungry as a kid."

"I think you're right," Gus said, smiling. "You boys certainly kept Rosa-Maria gainfully employed. She couldn't keep up with your growing appetites."

"Ever wonder why she stayed on after we all left home?" Luke asked quietly. He had his own suspicions about why Rosa-Maria continued to work at the ranch, but he would never voice those thoughts to his father. He doubted his old man had any interest in romance after being widowed once and divorced twice. Besides which, Luke would never do anything to jeopardize Rosa-Maria's employment.

Gus looked sharply at him as if he suspected it was a trick question. "I suspect she stays on because I pay her extremely well."

"Sure, Dad."

Luke took a long swallow of the sweet-tart lemonade and avoided his father's eyes. He was hardly the person to give anyone relationship advice, but he suspected Rosa-Maria was more than a little in love with his old man. Luke had only been home for six months, but he saw the way she looked at his dad when she thought nobody was watching. In her early sixties, she'd been a widow for more than thirty years. She was still an attractive woman, with long, black hair pulled back in a neat bun, and slight touches of gray at her temples. Her skin was smooth, and the only wrinkles were the laugh lines at the corners of her dark eyes.

"It's a good thing she did stay on," Gus continued, "considering all three of you are back under my roof and you're still eating me out of house and home."

But there was no rancor in his voice, and Luke knew his father was secretly pleased to have his three sons living and working at Riverrun Ranch. Even Emmaline had returned to Last Stand from New York City following her engagement to the former bull rider, Cort Channing. She'd found a job at an art gallery in town, and Gus had given her and Cort a plot of land on the western side of the ranch as an early wedding gift. For now, they were staying in the main house while they built a home on the property. The arrangement worked well, now that Cort and Holt were in business together.

But while Holt and Evan seemed content to live at the ranch and work the cattle, Luke felt restless. He loved the ranch, but he couldn't see himself living here forever.

He wanted something different.

Rosa-Maria came back onto the porch. "*Señor*, there is a phone call for you." Her gaze flicked to Luke and she gave Gus a meaningful look. "You should take it in your office."

Setting his lemonade down, Gus rose to his feet. "Thank you, Rosa-Maria. Excuse me, son, I need to take this call."

Luke frowned. "Everything okay?"

"Oh, sure." He gave Luke a wink. "Just business."

Luke watched, puzzled, as he disappeared into the house. His father rarely got involved in the running of the ranch, and the way he'd reacted to the phone call was definitely odd. Even more strange was the sense that both his father and Rosa-Maria didn't want him knowing who was calling.

Shrugging it off as his own overactive imagination, his thoughts turned again to Jorie Russell. There was something about her that roused his protective instincts. More than that, he found himself thinking about her in ways he hadn't allowed himself to think about any woman in a long time. She had real pretty eyes, and her hair reminded him of corn silk. He especially liked her long legs, and had caught himself wondering how they might feel wrapped around his waist.

Maybe it was time he found his own place, away from Riverrun Ranch. He had some money saved, enough to buy a piece of land and build a house. He needed to move on with his life. He wouldn't think of what he'd had with the army, or how much he'd looked forward to each day, working with Elsa. Those days were gone and, as much as he wished he could turn back time and redo that fateful day, he couldn't.

Chapter Five

J ORIE RECEIVED A call from McGuire's Garage early the
following morning that her car was ready. She thought
about calling either Jessie or Luke for a ride into town, but
finally opted to walk the two miles from her house to the
veterinary hospital, where she caught a ride into town with
Denise, a coworker who also helped care for the wildlife.

"You look exhausted." Denise glanced over at Jorie as
they drove.

"I am." She suppressed a yawn. "Mrs. Adams found three
baby squirrels in her shed two days ago. She left them alone
hoping the mother would return, but brought them to me
late yesterday afternoon when it became clear they'd been
abandoned. I was up most of the night, caring for them."

"How old are they?"

"Three or four days, I think. They're thin and they were
pretty dehydrated when they arrived. I didn't think they'd
make it through the night, but they did. I fed them just
before I left so they should be okay for a couple of hours."

The benefit of living so close to the veterinary hospital
was that she could zip home during the day to administer
feedings and medicine if she needed to. Several of her

coworkers also volunteered at the wildlife rehab center that she'd established out of her home. So far, she'd been lucky to have coverage during the times when she couldn't be there. She'd cut her hours at the clinic back to just three days a week, because so many animals were coming into the rehab center that required her attention. But the downside was that she was now making less money to finance their care.

"I worked the night shift last night and I have today off, so I'll go over and check on them later this morning," Denise offered.

"Would you? That would be great," Jorie said. "I'll run home at lunch, and I know Dr. Honeyman won't mind if I take a quick break in the afternoon."

Maybe one day she would go back to school and become a full-fledged vet herself, but she would need to save a lot of money, which was probably never going to happen.

Now they pulled up to McGuire's Garage. "Thanks for the ride, Denise, and for checking on the squirrels."

"Do you want me to wait for you?"

"No, that's okay." Jorie didn't want any witnesses if the repair cost was more than she could afford. "I'm all set now. Thanks again for the ride."

But when Matt McGuire handed her the invoice five minutes later, Jorie could only gape at him in surprise. "Are you sure this is all I owe you? This doesn't seem nearly enough, considering you had to tow it back here from downtown."

"Towing's free within five miles," Matt said, but he didn't meet her eyes. "It was just a bad spark plug. The whole thing took about ten minutes so I only charged you for the part and not the labor."

Jorie looked at him in suspicion, but he was searching for her car keys along a row of hooks and not looking at her. In the next instant, she chided herself for her skepticism. What possible reason would he have to lie to her about the work, or the price? The alternative was that Luke Claiborne had somehow convinced Matt to undercharge her.

And why would he do that?

The very thought was ridiculous. Luke barely knew her, and he certainly would have no reason to help her. She was being fanciful again, imagining that someone cared.

"Well, thank you," she finally said. She paid the bill and left a tip equal to the invoice amount in order to assuage the niggling guilt she felt that somehow she'd been given preferential treatment.

"You'll want to think about new tires sooner than later," Matt said as he returned her car keys. "The tread is all but gone, and the sidewalls are showing signs of wear."

He pointed out several areas that were cracked, and another tire that had a distinct bulge on the side. He was right, but she couldn't afford new tires. Her credit card was almost maxed out, and she needed to order supplies for her rescue animals. New tires would just have to wait until her next paycheck.

"I'll come back next week," she promised. "Somehow, I don't think new tires are going to be as affordable as a new spark plug."

She drove back through town, grateful the bill had been

so reasonable. Even better, the engine no longer sputtered, and the occasional knocking sound she'd become accustomed to had also vanished. Could a simple spark plug change really fix all those issues?

Glancing at her watch, she saw she still had twenty minutes before she needed to be at the clinic, which was more than enough time to grab a coffee at Java Time. She pulled into a parking spot in front of the café, eyeballing the expensive red sports car in the next spot. She didn't recognize the car, but Last Stand had plenty of wealthy tourists in town this time of year.

Inside the café, she placed her order and then stepped aside to wait, absently thumbing through the messages on her phone. She maintained a Facebook page for her wildlife rehab business, and had posted a photo of the baby squirrels when they'd come in last night. Tiny, hairless and pink, with their eyes still closed, they were nestled together on a soft fleece blanket. Already, she had more than sixty likes, and numerous comments on the photo. She looked up when the barista called her name, and gratefully accepted the latte she had ordered.

"Jorie? Jorie Russell?"

Jorie turned around at the sound of her name, and then froze when she saw who stood there, grinning at her as if he'd just won the lottery.

Mason Childress.

Her heart began to pound so hard in her chest, she thought for sure he must hear it, and her legs began to tremble in a way that had nothing to do with excitement, and everything to do with fear. Her fight-or-flight response was kicking in hard, and every instinct told her to *run*. She hadn't seen Mason in nine years, not since she'd been a naïve seventeen-year-old. She'd never been able to tell anyone about the night Mason assaulted her in his truck after offering her a ride home from a house party. Not even Luke Claiborne, yesterday, when he'd seemed so concerned and more than ready to help.

Now Mason was smiling at her like they were old friends and Jorie had to remind herself that they were standing in the middle of a busy coffee shop on a bright Monday morning. He couldn't hurt her. He couldn't intimidate her. He had no control over her.

So why was her entire body shaking?

She'd thought about this moment so many times since that night; had tried to imagine what it would be like to come face-to-face with her attacker again. In her imagination, she always had the upper hand and she always managed to humiliate him with her cutting words. In some of her fantasies, she even hurt him, physically. *He* was the reason she always carried a canister of pepper spray. If it hadn't been for Evan Claiborne, she was sure Mason would have raped her. As it was, he'd scared her more than she'd ever been scared in her life. Now she could only stare at him in mute dismay, as her heartbeat pounded in her eardrums.

He laughed and pulled an exaggerated expression of disbelief, opening his arms as if he might hug her. "What? You don't remember me? It's me . . . Mason!"

A part of her recognized that he was still an attractive

man, with reddish-brown hair and light-blue eyes. He'd put on a few pounds since she'd last seen him, and was thicker through the chest and middle. The extra weight was evident in his face too. His jawline had softened, but his eyes as he watched her were still sharp.

"I'm late for work," she said, her voice cold. She stepped past him out of the café and began walking swiftly toward her car. She couldn't believe he was back in town! The last she'd heard, he'd gotten some big-paying job with his father's fracking company and was living and working in Austin. She'd hoped never to see him again.

Ever.

"Hey, Jorie, hold on a sec." Mason followed her outside and as Jorie fumbled for her keys with fingers that trembled, he stood on the sidewalk, watching her. "What's your rush?"

"I told you, I'm late for work."

"Don't you even have time to say hello?"

"No." She didn't look at him. She wanted to tell him to go to hell, but she wasn't wired that way. Even though he didn't deserve a second of her time or consideration, she didn't have it in her to be blatantly rude to anyone. Not even Mason Childress. But as she tried to escape into her car, he stepped forward and put a hand on the door, preventing her from opening it. She stared at him in disbelief.

"C'mon, Jorie," he said in a cajoling tone. "Don't be like that. It's good to see you again. Maybe we could go out sometime and catch up. It'll be like old times." He made a little side-to-side movement, like a juggler. "We did have some good times, right?"

Good times? *He had tried to rape her.* If Evan Claiborne hadn't chosen that moment to open the door to Mason's truck and interrupt what was happening, Jorie was certain there would have been a very different end to the story.

"Go to hell, Mason. And let go of my door. Or maybe I should get one of the Claiborne brothers over here. You remember Evan Claiborne, right?"

She couldn't believe she'd actually said the words, but the instant they were out of her mouth, she felt empowered by her own chutzpah.

Mason put his hands up in mock surrender and took a step back. "Okay, okay, no need to get your panties in a twist."

Jorie yanked the door open, and was preparing to jump in when a pickup truck that had been driving past suddenly slowed and came to a stop directly behind her car.

"Hey, Jorie, everything okay?"

She looked up to see Luke Claiborne leaning across the seat to peer at her through the open passenger window. She couldn't believe his timing, given what she had just said to Mason.

She gave a jerky nod, grateful for his sudden appearance. "Yes, I was just heading to work."

"Okay." His eyes flicked to Mason, still standing too close, but he didn't acknowledge the other man, even though they were the same age and must have known each other growing up. "Glad to see you got your car back. How is it running?"

"Good, thanks."

"Great. I'll see you later." He gave Mason one last look, and then drove slowly away.

As Jorie quickly climbed into her car and locked the door, Mason walked over to the sleek, red sports car and lit a cigarette, watching her through a plume of white smoke as she turned the ignition and put the car into reverse. Jorie barely suppressed a snort of disgust. Of course he drove something ostentatious and expensive. He'd always worn his father's money on his sleeve, making sure everyone in town knew who he was. He'd always believed his family's wealth made him better than everyone else. Certainly better than a girl from the wrong side of Hickory Creek.

As she backed out of the parking spot and drove through town, she was gratified when Luke's big truck pulled onto the street behind her. He followed her all the way to the veterinary clinic, raising a hand in farewell as she turned into the parking lot. Killing the engine, she sat for a moment, considering the events of the morning.

She still couldn't believe Mason was back in Last Stand, although she shouldn't be so surprised. His parents still owned a house in town even though they rarely spent time there. So, why had Mason returned? Seeing him again brought all the ugly memories of that awful night rushing back.

She'd never told anyone what had happened, not even Callie, who had been at the party with her. Not even Jessie. She'd made Evan swear never to tell anyone either. At first he'd refused, determined to bring her to the police station to report the attack. She'd begged him not to. She was too ashamed, because a tiny part of her believed it might have been her own fault. She shouldn't have been at that stupid party in the first place, and she definitely shouldn't have been drinking, but she'd wanted so badly to fit in, to be one of the cool kids. She'd been a little awestruck when Mason Childress singled her out for his attentions, plying her with alcohol and compliments, and treating her as if she was the most fascinating girl at the party. She certainly hadn't done anything to rebuff him. At twenty-one, he'd been way too old for her, but she'd been more than a little overwhelmed by his collegiate good looks and—yes, she could admit it— the fact that he belonged to one of Last Stand's wealthiest families. So when she'd begun to feel sick and unsteady on her feet, she'd been grateful for his offer to drive her home.

Jorie didn't want to remember what had happened after she'd gotten into his truck. She still had a hard time understanding how a guy so seemingly *normal* could be such a monster in reality. Mason hadn't even driven her away from the party; he'd simply attacked her right there in the driveway, in the cab of his truck. When she'd fought back, he'd struck her hard across the face. She'd been helpless against his superior strength, and had actually sobbed with relief when Evan Claiborne had suddenly wrenched the driver's door open and hauled Mason out of the truck. Granted, he'd been looking for his sister, Callie, but Jorie would always be grateful for his timely intervention. He'd taken one look at her tearful face and crumpled clothing and had punched Mason.

Hard.

As he'd half-carried her over to his own truck, she'd begged him not to tell anyone. He'd been so furious; so unlike the easygoing Evan she was accustomed to. But he knew as well as she did what would happen if she reported the incident. With his money and influence, Mason's father would make sure the accusation went nowhere. At worst, she would be victimized again in court, and the Childress family would make her life miserable.

In the end, Evan had unwillingly agreed to keep her secret. Then he'd collected Callie and had driven Jorie home. He hadn't said anything to her during the drive to Hickory Creek Road. Callie had been too busy begging Evan not to tell her father they'd been drinking to even notice Jorie's misery. A part of her knew she should report the incident. Mason had assaulted her. He'd left bruises and had bloodied her nose when he'd hit her. If not for Evan, he would have done worse. But she'd never reported it because even her own grandmother, who had been waiting for her when she arrived home that night, disheveled, drunk, and deeply traumatized, hadn't believed her story. She'd blamed Jorie, claiming she'd *asked* for it by wearing a skimpy dress. She'd said the apple hadn't fallen far from the tree.

If her own grandmother wouldn't believe her, why would anyone else? People would say she was just like her mother—promiscuous and wild. And there was no way she would involve Evan.

He probably blamed her too.

They'd never talked about it again and, as far as she knew, he'd kept his promise and never told anyone about the incident.

Shaking off the disturbing memories, Jorie climbed out of the car. Seeing Mason Childress had reminded her of two truths—even outwardly good men could hide a dark side, and she had no business thinking she could start a relationship with Luke Claiborne. She was too damaged, and she didn't know Luke well enough to trust him.

Chapter Six

SEEING MASON CHILDRESS had irritated the shit out of Luke. He'd been driving through town when he'd spotted Jorie's little SUV parked in front of the coffee shop. Knowing she'd likely be inside Java Time, he'd swung his truck around at the next intersection and headed back, intending to grab a coffee for himself and maybe say hello to her. Only she'd been standing by the driver's door of her car and Mason had been *looming* over her. There was no other way to describe it. Luke could read body language, and Mason's had screamed intimidation, while Jorie's . . . She'd put on a good show, but she'd been terrified.

Luke had never liked Mason. Maybe he wasn't being fair, but there was something about the guy that rubbed him the wrong way. His brothers would say he was just jealous of all that Childress money, but Luke knew it went beyond that.

He'd heard the rumors.

Mason had been expelled from the expensive prep school he'd attended in Austin, but that hadn't prevented him from getting accepted into a fancy college on the East Coast. But he'd dropped out—or had been kicked out—in his junior year. He'd come back to Last Stand, presumably to learn the family business, instead.

Luke wasn't buying it.

The way he figured, Mason's old man had dropped close to half a million dollars on his son's education. Why would he allow the kid to quit when he was so close to the finish line? Something didn't add up. Quite frankly, Luke didn't care about Mason Childress and what he did or didn't do in college. But if Mason threatened Jorie in any way, he considered that his business. He wouldn't stand by and watch him bully anyone.

Now it was nearly dinnertime, and he was heading back to the ranch after having picked up a load of supplies from the local feed and grain. As he neared Hickory Creek, some impulse had him turning to drive past the veterinary clinic. He had no idea if Jorie would still be at work, but a quick glance at the parking lot told him her car was gone. Feeling a little foolish, he decided to take the long way back to River-run.

The roads on the outskirts of town were pot-holed and sparsely populated. Every so often, he would pass a gated driveway with the name of the family ranch overhead: Rough Hollow Ranch, Rivers Bend Ranch, and Three Sisters Ranch. They were all familiar landmarks, even if he no longer knew the families the way he had when he'd been a kid. Even so, he considered the town of Last Stand to be a tight-knit community. After all, hadn't they gotten their start back in the 1830's by standing together against a contingent of the Mexican army? Despite the odds, the people who had lived in this area way back then had holed themselves up in the saloon and held off the Mexican army for three days. Finally, the Mexicans had conceded defeat and moved on to easier targets, and the town of Last Stand had been born. Luke was pretty proud of the fact that he was descended from one of those brave men, Sherman "Shotgun" Claiborne.

Luke was so lost in his thoughts that he almost didn't see the little silver SUV until he'd passed it. Pulled off into the trees on the side of the road, it was definitely Jorie's car, but there was no sign of her. Frowning, Luke pulled his truck in behind hers and killed the engine. As he did so, Jorie stood up from where she'd been crouched on the passenger side of the car, and Luke saw the relief that flashed across her features. Her blond hair was pulled back in a ponytail and she still wore her clinic scrubs, this time in a shade of pale lavender.

"Oh, thank goodness it's you!" she exclaimed, as he climbed out of the truck and approached her.

"Everything okay?" he asked.

"Well, no . . . not exactly."

She stepped back as he rounded the side of the car, and he saw her front tire was completely flat.

"Looks like the sidewall blew out," Luke said, bending down to examine the tire.

"I hit a pothole and it just sort of . . . popped!" She looked sheepish. "Matt at the garage warned me that the tires needed to be replaced, but I thought it could wait until next week."

"Yeah, no worries," Luke assured her. She had a smudge

of grime on her cheek, and he had an urge to wipe it away with his thumb. He pushed his hands into his pockets instead. "I can change the tire for you, and follow you back to town. Looks like your other tires need replacing too. Maybe Matt can do that for you tomorrow."

Without waiting for her response, he walked around to the back of the SUV, to retrieve the spare tire.

"Luke, wait—"

Opening the hatch, he took a hasty step back, and stared in dismay at the little creature looking up at him.

"There's a fucking *skunk* in your car!"

Laughing, Jorie came to stand beside him. "Relax, she's just a baby. She won't be able to spray for at least another month, so you're safe."

"Thanks, good to know." Then, looking past the crate that housed the skunk, he saw more eyes peering through the wire grate of a second crate. "Are those raccoons?"

"Yes, three of them," Jorie said. "The skunk kit was brought into the clinic today, but we don't treat wildlife, so I agreed to bring it home and care for it there. Then, just as I was leaving, I got a call about three baby raccoons living under someone's front steps, but the mother hadn't been seen in days. So I drove out and picked them up, and was on my way home when I hit the pothole."

Luke stared her in disbelief. "You're going to care for these critters at your *house*?"

"Of course." She sounded indignant. "That's what I do. I'm a certified wildlife rehabber. They'll be cared for indoors until they're strong enough to be transferred to the outdoor enclosures. When they're finally big enough, they'll be released back into the wild."

"How come I didn't know this?" Luke was surprised that neither his father nor Rosa-Maria had mentioned Jorie's wildlife rehabbing efforts. "I thought you just rescued feral cats and shit."

Jorie frowned at him. "Do you have to swear so much?"

Luke ignored the comment. He didn't know why, but he found he swore more when he was around her than when he was with anyone else. "Aren't you afraid of contracting rabies?"

Jorie gave him a tolerant look. "No."

"Okay, well, help me move these crates out of the car. The spare tire must be underneath the floor."

As he reached for the first crate, hoping Jorie was right about the skunk being too young to spray, she reached over and forestalled him with one hand on his arm. "Um, don't bother. There is no spare tire."

"Why not?"

"I took it out so I could store extra supplies in that space." Seeing his expression, her own grew defensive. "Don't look at me that way."

"Seriously," he all but growled, "you have absolutely no sense of self-preservation. You could have been out here all fucking night if I hadn't come along."

She frowned at his use of the F-bomb, but didn't chastise him. "I would have called Jessie."

"There's no cell phone reception out here. You wouldn't have reached anyone."

"Then I would have walked to the next ranch and used their phone. Really, Luke, you're making too big a deal out of this. But I do appreciate your concern, and I am glad you came along when you did."

She'd never called him by his name before, and Luke realized he liked the way it sounded when she said it. But he didn't like thinking about her out here, alone. Maybe she could have walked to the nearest ranch, and maybe Last Stand was a safe, small town, but it'd be dark soon and this was such a remote area.

"Okay, let's get these crates into my truck," he said. "I'll give you a lift home. If you still have the spare lying around, I'll come back and change the tire."

He let Jorie take the crate with the baby skunk, and he took the larger crate with the three little raccoons. They peered at him with their bright, black eyes, and he had to admit, they were pretty cute.

"I just have to grab some stuff from the car," Jorie said, after the crates were secured in the bed of the truck.

Luke waited while she retrieved her belongings and locked the car, before he handed her up into the passenger side of the cab. As she stepped past him, he caught a whiff of her scent, something light and floral that reminded him of summer days and fields of wildflowers. She didn't look at him as she settled into the passenger seat, and he noticed how she held her large tote bag on her lap, clutching it against her body like a shield.

"Buckle up," he said, his voice gruffer than he intended. Whenever she was in the truck with him, she acted as if she expected him to pounce on her. Maybe he'd been too harsh with her that first time he'd encountered her, behind the warehouse. As much as he hated the thought, maybe he'd frightened her. He made a mental note to tone down his language when she was around.

As he turned the truck around and headed in the direction of her house, he could almost sense when she began to relax. Reaching out, she touched the photo of himself and Elsa that he kept on the dash.

"Was this your military dog?"

"That's Elsa," he said. "She was my partner."

"What happened to her?"

Luke heard the trepidation in Jorie's voice, as if she was afraid to hear the answer.

"She's fine. She was reassigned to a new soldier and last I heard, she deployed to Afghanistan with him."

Jorie gave a soft exclamation. "But isn't that hard for the dog? I mean, how long did you two work together?"

Luke lifted one shoulder. "We were together for five years. But the military invested a lot of money in her training and technically, she's still active duty."

"Will you ever see her again?"

"I hope so. When it comes time for her to retire, I'll be given first dibs to adopt her since I was her first handler. If I choose not to take her, then one of her other handlers will have that choice or she could be adopted out to a civilian family."

"When will she be eligible for retirement?"

"She's seven years old, so I expect she'll be ready in about a year or so. That's about the age most military dogs retire."

One more year. It seemed like an eternity, but Luke looked forward to the day when he could bring Elsa home as a member of the family. She'd never need to work again. He'd make sure her days entailed nothing more strenuous than chasing a ball across the grass, or sniffing out a squirrel.

"I'm sorry," Jorie said. "That must have been hard to leave her behind when you got out."

"It was tough, yeah." Luke had never talked about Elsa with his family. His father and Holt had met her when he'd graduated from Military Police School, but he wasn't sure they understood the depth of his bond with his dog, or how much they had relied on one another.

Or how much Luke missed her.

Now he sought to move the conversation to safer ground. "Did you know all working dogs are trained right here in Texas?"

"No, I had no idea. Where?"

"Lackland Air Force Base in San Antonio has an extensive training school, and every dog in law enforcement goes through their program, whether they're civilian or military."

"Really! That's amazing. How do they get the dogs?" Jorie asked. "Do people just bring them puppies, or do they breed them there?"

"They do have a breeding program," Luke acknowledged, "but they still get a percentage of their dogs from Belgium and Germany."

"So what happens to the dogs that don't meet the standards, or who fail out of the program? Not all puppies make suitable working dogs, right? Please tell me they're not euthanized."

Jorie sounded so concerned that Luke had an urge to reach over and cover her hand with his own. But he didn't. He knew he made her nervous, and he didn't want to see her cringing away from him.

"No dogs are euthanized," he reassured her. "About fifty percent of the dogs fail out of the training, and they're all adopted out to good homes."

"That's good," she said, smiling in relief. "She's a beautiful dog. I hope I get to meet her one day."

"Yeah, me too," Luke replied.

They were driving on Hickory Creek Road and as they drew closer to Jorie's house, they saw a car on the side of the road. A flashy red sports car.

"Expecting company?" Luke asked, and cast a sideways glance at Jorie. Her face had blanched and she was staring at the car with something like loathing.

"No."

Before they reached Jorie's driveway, the car pulled onto the road and accelerated swiftly until it finally vanished around a bend. Beside him, Jorie expelled a pent-up breath. Luke recognized the car as Mason's. But why had he been stopped at Jorie's driveway?

"Everything okay?" he asked.

She gave him a quick, false smile. "Of course."

"Any idea why Mason Childress would be snooping around out here?" The Childress house was on the opposite side of town, on a pretty piece of property that put the

Claiborne ranch to shame.

"I have no idea what he was doing or why," Jorie said stiffly. "We barely know each other."

"How do you know him at all?" Luke knew it was none of his business, but he didn't like the fact that Mason had been lurking around. He neither liked the other man, nor trusted him. "He's a bit older than you, isn't he?"

Jorie shrugged. "I met him once, years ago. He was home from college and—" She made an impatient gesture. "Look, it doesn't matter. It's a free world and if he wants to drive around out here, who cares?"

They had reached her mailbox, and Luke turned down her driveway. He glanced at Jorie. Her expression was tight, and she had the tote bag clenched in her hands again. He knew if it hadn't been for the two crates in the bed of his truck, he'd have never made it down the driveway.

"I'll help you bring the crates inside," he offered.

"Really, there's no need. I can manage."

Luke pulled the truck up to the front of the mobile home and turned off the engine. Twisting in his seat, he faced Jorie. "Listen, I'm not going to leave you to manage those crates on your own. I'm guessing that you don't want me to see where you live, but I'm telling you right now, you have nothing to be ashamed of."

Jorie was looking down at her hands, still clasped around the handle of her tote bag. When she spoke, her voice was so low that he had to bend toward her to hear her words. "I'm not ashamed."

"Then why do I get the distinct sense you'd have preferred I dropped you off back by the road?"

She gave a non-committal shrug. "Because I know what you're accustomed to, and this must seem pretty pathetic by comparison. Also, I know what they say about the people who live on the other side of Hickory Creek."

"Jorie, look at me."

She did, slowly and reluctantly.

"You've overcome some pretty big obstacles in your life, and you've done an amazing job," he said. "You should be proud of yourself. I mean, look at what you've accomplished . . . you're a vet tech and a wildlife rehabber! You're smart and compassionate, and everyone in town seems to know and like you. You're living out here on your own, and you're making a difference in the lives of the animals you care for. You've got nothing to feel ashamed about."

A smile twitched at the corner of her mouth. "Thank you. Although you did say I have no sense of self-preservation. Twice, as I recall."

Luke grinned, relieved that she seemed to be lightening up. "Well, that's true. Which is why it's a good thing you have me. Speaking of which, where is the spare tire? I'll throw it in my truck before I leave."

"It's in the shed." Her face twisted into an expression of uncertainty. "Are you sure you don't mind doing that?"

"I seriously don't mind," he assured her, and realized it was true. Something about her sweet earnestness made him want to do nice things for her. "If you want to go back with me, you can wait while I change the tire, and then drive the car back here. At least then you'll have it for the morning.

But promise me you'll take it over to McGuire's Garage first thing."

"Okay," she said, and blew out a hard breath. "I was hoping I could hold out until I get paid, but I guess I can put it on my card."

"Yeah, the tires can't wait, Jorie. I'll stop by the garage in the morning and talk with Matt, see what he can do in the way of prices. Maybe he has some retreads he can use, which would work just as well, but cost less."

Her gaze sharpened on him and her eyes narrowed in suspicion. "By the way, my previous engine trouble only cost me twenty dollars. Matt said it was just a spark plug that needed replacing. Does that sound right to you?"

Luke shrugged. "He's the mechanic, not me."

"So you wouldn't have negotiated a lower price for me, right?"

She was perceptive. He'd have to be careful. He shook his head. "Nope. I have no idea why you would think that. But I'm happy to talk tires with Matt in the morning."

"Thank you." She smiled, apparently satisfied he was telling the truth. "That would mean a lot to me."

"Sure."

Abruptly, he got out of the truck and went around to the back to lower the tailgate. Her smile did funny things to him, and if he wasn't careful, he'd find himself volunteering to pay for her new tires. He wouldn't mind doing that for her, and he could easily afford to, but he knew she wouldn't appreciate the offer. But damned if there wasn't something about Jorie Russell that made him *want* to do nice things for her, because when she smiled at him like that, he felt like a fucking superhero.

He heard her door open and she came around to stand beside him. Luke didn't look at her, but instead bent his attention to unfastening the straps that he'd used to secure the crates.

"Are these going in the house?" he asked.

"Yes." She hitched her tote bag over one shoulder and reached for the crate containing the baby skunk. "Here, I'll take that one."

"Why don't you get the door, and I'll carry the crates." He lifted both crates easily, and waited while she stood indecisively.

"Fine."

Turning on her heel, she preceded him up the ramp to the front door of the mobile home. Luke followed, admiring the sweet curve of her ass that even the work scrubs couldn't disguise. He waited while she unlocked the door and then stepped inside. Luke had to turn sideways to manage the two crates, and then he found himself in a small, but surprisingly modern, kitchen. It looked to have been renovated fairly recently, with bright, white cupboards and a pretty glass backsplash over the sink and stove. A small table and two chairs sat in front of a large bay window, and everywhere, there were small, feminine touches.

"You can bring those crates through here," Jorie said, indicating a wide door at the far end of the kitchen.

"Right." Luke nodded, and followed her.

The entire middle section of the mobile home had been

converted into an animal clinic. Luke set the crates down on the tile floor and stared around in amazement. For a moment, he thought he'd walked into a pet shop. One wall of the room was lined, floor to ceiling, with metal cages, one on top of the other, occupied by animals of all breeds and sizes. On the opposite side of the room stood several shelves stocked with supplies. A modern incubator sat on a rolling steel table, and a half dozen intravenous poles stood against the wall. A small kitchenette had been built in the far corner, complete with a counter and a large sink, and refrigerator. Overhead cupboards were labeled with lists of medications and supplies. He retracted his earlier assessment; this room was a working veterinary clinic, not a pet store.

What looked to have been a dining nook was now an office, of sorts. There was a modern-looking desk with a laptop and two enormous monitors, filing cabinets, and a landline telephone. Beside the desk was a cot, with bedding and a pillow neatly folded and stacked at the foot. A narrow hallway extended beyond the clinic to the back of the mobile home, where he guessed the bathroom and bedrooms were located.

"Thanks," Jorie said, watching him. "I can take it from here."

"Is that where you sleep?" he asked in dismay, indicating the cot.

"What? Oh, no." She smiled. "That's for our volunteers. Sometimes we have so many critical-care patients that I need someone to help out overnight."

No wonder she couldn't afford new tires. From the look

of the clinic, she sank every extra penny she had into caring for the animals.

"I'm impressed with what you've done in here. I don't think I had an appreciation for just how big an operation this is."

Jorie shrugged, but he thought she looked pleased. "I just wish I could do more. Speaking of which, these little guys need to be evaluated so I can begin getting them healthy again." She hesitated. "Do you want me to show you where the spare tire is?"

"Yeah, sure," he said. "Why don't I go change the tire and bring your car back for you? That way, you can just focus on your work here."

"Really? You would do that for me?"

"Sure."

"But how will you get back to your truck? How will you get home?"

"I'll call Evan and ask him to pick me up. It's not an issue."

This time, the smile she gave him set alarm bells off in his head. He had no business feeling so pleased about the fact that he'd made her happy. He'd need to be careful; a guy could get addicted to that kind of wattage.

He followed her outside and around to the back of the trailer, to a large shed. While Jorie worked the padlock, he stared at the enclosures someone had built, using two-by-fours and chicken wire. There were two of them, and even from a distance, he could see one pen housed raccoons, while two small red foxes circled the interior of the second one.

Intrigued, he walked closer and watched the raccoons as they played. Someone had suspended a cloth hammock from an overhead timber, and as three of the raccoons climbed inside, he noticed how the timber bowed, and two of the side supports pulled inward. Examining the supports, he realized they were beginning to rot at the bottom. Curious, he checked the remaining supports, and found the same issue.

"How long have these enclosures been here?" he asked, walking back to where Jorie stood inside the door of the shed, watching him.

"Maybe eight years? I hired a local guy to build them after my grandmother passed.

Why?"

Luke shook his head. "No reason. Here, let me get the spare tire, and I'll be on my way. You're sure you don't need any help with the skunk and the raccoons? You're okay handling them by yourself?"

She gave him a wry smile. "Completely sure. If there's one thing I've learned since I've been on my own, it's how to handle animals."

Luke hefted the spare tire and made his way to his pickup truck, considering her words. Why did he have the unsettling sense that she wasn't only referring to the four-legged kind?

Chapter Seven

JORIE WAITED UNTIL the big pickup truck disappeared from view before she collapsed weakly against the side of the shed. Luke Claiborne seemed to have that effect on her. He was quickly becoming her knight in shining armor, but her feelings about being rescued by him—twice now, three times if you counted the day she'd had the run-in with Mason—were all mixed up. She'd looked out for herself for so long, she'd forgotten what it was like to have someone to lean on. What had he said, exactly?

It's a good thing you have me.

Another girl might read more into those words than he'd intended. But she was Jorie Russell, the girl from the wrong side of the creek. If nothing else, she was a realist. She didn't *have* Luke Claiborne any more than she had a chance of winning the lottery.

With a sigh, she straightened, locked the shed, and trudged back to the house. She had a long night ahead of her, ensuring her new patients were properly treated and settled into their temporary homes. She still had to feed the raccoons and the foxes, and then begin the nightly routine of feeding the baby squirrels and tending to the dozens of other small animals in her care. And when she finished doing all of that, she needed to post new photos to the Facebook page she'd created, and send out a plea to her followers for more supplies. Her bills were mounting and it wouldn't be long before she'd no longer be able to afford the medicine and equipment she needed. She hated to think about closing the rehab center, but acknowledged she might not have a choice.

But no sooner did she lift the tiny skunk out of its crate and feel it nestle into her palms, so helpless and trusting, she knew she would do whatever it took to keep her small operation running. She had too many lives depending on her for their very survival, and she wouldn't fail them.

JORIE WAS AWAKENED the following morning by the sound of a power saw, so loud and strident that she found herself out of bed and standing in the kitchen before she was even fully awake. The sun had barely risen, but the racket continued. Rubbing her bleary eyes, she turned on the light over the small kitchen table and peered at the clock on the oven. It was just seven o'clock and since she didn't have to work at the veterinary clinic that day, she'd been looking forward to sleeping in, just a little bit longer than usual.

Pushing back the curtain over the front window, she peered out at the driveway, surprised to see both her SUV and two pickup trucks parked there, one of them with a flatbed trailer hooked to the tow hitch. From behind the house, she could hear the sound of a tractor, and the whine of a power saw.

What the heck?

Jorie opened the back door and stood for a moment, staring in dismay. Her backyard looked like a construction site, with piles of lumber and large coils of wire fencing stacked to one side. A cement mixer slowly churned near her shed, and Luke Claiborne was using a hand saw to cut a thick board. His brother Evan had apparently dug up the grass and topsoil in a long, rectangular area near the enclosures, and was now grading it with a small front loader.

"What are you doing?" she shouted, but neither man heard her, nor even noticed her.

With a sound of frustration and heedless of her bare feet or the fact she still wore her pajamas, Jorie clambered down the rickety steps and across the dewy grass to stand in front of the sawhorses where Luke worked the power saw. But it wasn't until she waved her arms in his line of vision that he finally saw her. He turned off the tool and set it aside, before lifting the goggles he wore to the top of his head. His dark eyes slid over her in a way that made Jorie realize just how little she wore in the way of clothing. Ignoring the urge to cross her arms over her chest, she swept one hand wide, indicating the array of tools and equipment.

"What are you doing?" she demanded.

"What does it look like?" He grinned, and there was no mistaking the male appreciation in his eyes as he watched her.

"Nobody gave you permission to do this," she spluttered, refusing to be distracted by his good looks, or the way his smile made her heart beat faster. "I never asked you to do this."

Glancing at Evan, who wore safety earmuffs and was unaware Jorie had come outside, Luke stepped out from behind the sawhorse. He unbuckled the leather tool belt that rode low on his hips and draped it over the board he'd been cutting. "Do you have any fresh coffee?"

"What?" Jorie stared at him in bemusement, too absorbed in how good he looked wearing that tool belt to fully comprehend his question.

"Coffee," Luke repeated, his eyes gleaming. "Do you have any?"

"No. I mean, I literally just woke up! Because of your racket, I might add. And by the way, the sound of that saw nearly scared me to death. S o no, I haven't had a chance to make any coffee yet."

"Let's go take care of that," he said, and before Jorie had a chance to protest, he removed his gloves, took her by the arm and walked her back toward the house. "What are you doing out here in your bare feet, anyway? You could have stepped on a nail or, even worse, a snake."

Jorie tried to ignore how warm his hand felt around her arm and how good he smelled, like clean soap and freshly cut wood. But there was no ignoring the bright burst of awareness that sparkled through her like a fizzy Coke, full of sugar and joy.

"All the noise is frightening the animals," she protested, looking over her shoulder at the two enclosures, where neither the raccoons nor the foxes were to be seen.

"They'll survive," he said calmly, opening the back door and ushering her into the trailer.

"Why aren't you wearing any ear protection?" Jorie asked. "You're going to damage your hearing."

But Luke had already turned away, and didn't respond. Leaving her standing in the middle of the kitchen, he began opening cupboards and drawers until he found her coffee, and then deftly began brewing a pot, scooping spoonfuls of fragrant grounds into a filter. Glancing at her, he nodded his chin toward the rear of the trailer.

"Go get dressed, I'll make coffee."

Realizing she wore only a pair of shorts and an oversized T-shirt, and that her hair was likely a disaster, she scooted out of the kitchen and through the clinic to her bedroom, where she caught sight of herself in the mirror.

"Oh, no, no," she moaned softly, and swiftly drew a brush through the tangled mass of her hair, before pulling it back into a smooth ponytail.

A plaintive *meow* drew her attention to a large cardboard box beside the bed where Taco, the mother cat they had rescued from the warehouse fire, lay inside with her three kittens. Bending down, Jorie stroked the cat beneath her chin and was reward by her loud purr.

"How're you, my sweet girl?" Jorie murmured. She gently stroked each of the kittens in turn. Their eyes had finally opened, but their vision was still poor. Jorie watched them for a moment as they climbed clumsily over each other in search of their mother. She'd already begun the process of finding permanent homes for each of them, just as soon as they were ready. "Soon," she said softly, "you'll each have your forever homes."

Quickly, she scrubbed her face and pulled on a pair of blue jeans. She automatically reached for a clean, plain T-shirt, but then paused and reached instead for a pretty floral blouse with a deep V-neck and no sleeves. Slipping her feet into a pair of sandals, she viewed her reflection. She looked pale, but she would do.

As she made her way through the clinic, she checked on each of her patients, noting with satisfaction that both the baby skunk and the squirrels were sleeping comfortably. She'd have a quick cup of coffee while Luke explained what he was doing on her property, and then she would begin the daily routine of feedings, cleanings, and meds. But when she walked back into the kitchen, Luke stood at her small stove, expertly flipping eggs in one pan while bacon sizzled in a second.

"What are you doing?" she asked in dismay.

"I'm cooking breakfast." He glanced at her over his shoulder and then did a quick double take. He didn't say anything, but Jorie was suddenly glad she'd chosen the pretty, sleeveless blouse over the T-shirt. "You look like you could use something substantial to eat."

Okay, so maybe he hadn't been admiring her, as she'd thought. Feeling disgruntled, she poured herself a cup of coffee and leaned against the counter to watch him. He seemed completely at home, and even the frilly blue apron he'd tied around his waist couldn't detract from his utter manliness.

"You didn't have to do this," she murmured, as he deftly scooped two eggs and some bacon onto a plate and handed it to her.

Before he could reply, the door opened and Evan poked his head into the trailer. "I knew I smelled bacon. You two holding out on me?"

Luke slanted a rueful grin at Jorie. "The guy has a nose like a bloodhound."

"Do you have enough for me?" Evan peered over his brother's shoulder. "Oh, yeah, plenty to go around!"

Jorie sat down with her plate and her coffee, and waited as Luke prepared two more plates. He handed one to Evan and then pulled out the only remaining chair and sat down across from Jorie, while Evan leaned against the counter and dug into his meal with appreciation.

"If there's one thing Luke can do right, it's breakfast," Evan said around a mouthful.

Luke paused, his fork halfway to his mouth, and pinned his brother with a meaningful look. "Oh, there are lots of things I can do right," he said, "but you'll never know."

Evan laughed and nodded. "Okay, bro. If you say so. Let me just say I haven't seen any evidence to support your claim."

His expression was one of rich amusement as his gaze slid momentarily to Jorie, and she had the distinct sense there was a private joke in there somewhere, one she probably didn't want to know anything about.

"So," she said, when they were almost finished eating. "Breakfast was delicious, thank you. But what did I do to deserve it, and what the heck are you doing to my backyard?"

Evan gulped the rest of his coffee and set his dishes in the sink. "I think that's my cue to leave. Jorie, all I ask is, don't kill him, because I need his help mending fences along the south ridge tomorrow."

After Evan had disappeared outside, Luke gathered up the dishes. He put them in the sink and filled it with hot, soapy water.

"You're not going to escape answering by washing the dishes," she said, her tone wry.

"Seems to me you have a lot on your plate, and not many helping hands," he finally said, turning to face her. "Those enclosures were probably fine when they were first built— what, ten years ago, you said?"

"Almost. I think it's been about eight years."

"The support posts are beginning to rot at the ground level, Jorie. If one of them goes over, it wouldn't take much for your animals to get loose. I also noticed where one of the foxes is digging below the fence. I checked this morning, and that wire doesn't extend down far enough. I'm actually surprised none of your critters haven't already tunneled its way out."

Jorie knew everything he said was true; she'd already noted the deteriorating condition of the enclosures, and repairing them was on her long list of things to do around the place, but she didn't have the resources.

"But none of that is your problem," she persisted. "So why are you doing it?"

"Why not?" he asked. "Can't someone do something

nice just because they want to? Or are you the only one allowed to do that?"

Jorie frowned. "No, of course not—"

"Good. Then it's settled. Evan and I are going to build a new enclosure for your raccoons, with a poured concrete floor. We'll build a second pen for the foxes and we'll shore up the existing pen until we can get some more permanent repairs done. When we're finished, you'll have three strong, outdoor areas."

"I—I can't pay you," she mumbled.

"Sorry, what was that?"

She looked sharply at him. "I said I can't pay you. At least not right away."

"I'm not doing it because I expect you to pay me, Jorie." His voice was infinitely patient. "I'm doing it because you're a family friend and you could use a hand."

Of course. She was a family friend. Why else would he go to all this trouble and expense? Jorie pushed down her disappointment. She should be grateful for everything he was doing. She had no right to expect more.

"Well, you must have paid a fortune for all the materials," she protested. "I don't know . . . it doesn't feel right."

"Most of it's excess stuff we had hanging around the ranch," he assured her. "Trust me, it will never be missed."

Jorie narrowed her eyes at him, hating herself for asking, but knowing she would just the same. She'd learned early on there was no such thing as a free lunch. "So what's the catch?"

"There is no catch."

"So you don't expect *anything* in return?"

"Let's just say, I don't want anything you're not ready to give me," he said, his expression fathomless.

He left Jorie standing in the kitchen, floundering for words. Had he actually meant what she thought he'd meant? She'd had a crush on him for as long as she could remember, but she'd never actually allowed her imagination to travel *there*. She'd never let herself imagine anything overtly physical. Just the thought of Luke touching her or kissing her made her feel all hot and shivery at the same time. She didn't even know if she could be intimate with anyone, after what had happened to her.

What if she freaked out on him?

What if she was frigid?

And why had he said he didn't want anything she wasn't ready to give? Was there an underlying meaning in his words? Did he know she was damaged? Flawed? That she'd never been with a man?

Scrubbing her hands over her face, Jorie groaned in despair. She didn't know if she had the courage to put herself out there. Did she dare?

Moving to the window, she stood watching Luke as he worked. She could hear him laughing at something Evan said, and as he lifted the saw and bent over the wood, his muscles strained and bulged beneath his T-shirt. The morning sun washed over his black hair like liquid, making it look as sleek and smooth as a raven's wing. His movements were deft and easy, and she recalled again how gently he had handled the kittens.

She remembered he'd been a K9 handler in the army. She knew a little about working dogs, and becoming a handler required months of training and the ability to maintain control under any and all circumstances. A K9 handler had to be both mentally and physically fit, which gave Jorie a certain sense of reassurance. Luke wouldn't be abusive. In fact, she had no reason to think he would ever— could ever—behave like Mason Childress. Everything she'd seen indicated he was the complete opposite of a man like Mason in every way.

Jorie washed the breakfast dishes and put them away, before moving into the clinic to begin her morning routine of caring for her four-legged patients. Outside, she could hear Luke and Evan talking, their masculine voices raised over the sound of hammering and circular saws. Knowing they were giving both their time and energy to improve her situation was both humbling and heartening.

She spent several moments preparing formula for the baby squirrels and the skunk, and assembling nuts, grains, and various fruits and vegetables for the older animals. Reaching into the nearest cage, she gently drew out the first baby squirrel, holding it in her gloved hand as she tempted it with a syringe filled with formula. After a moment, the squirrel grasped the end of the syringe with its tiny paws and drank greedily.

Jorie smiled. "Sometimes we all need a helping hand, right, little guy?" she crooned.

As she placed the sated infant back into the cage and carefully picked up the second squirrel, she realized that for the first time in a long time, she felt hope.

Chapter Eight

MORNING SUNLIGHT SLANTED through the trees behind Riverrun Ranch and dappled the patio in a mosaic of light. Luke finished his breakfast and gulped down the last bit of coffee in his cup. Pushing his chair back, he was just getting ready to leave when his father appeared. He looked crisp in a black western shirt with pearl snaps, and a pair of black Wranglers with a silver belt buckle. His blue eyes brightened when he saw Luke.

"Ah, I see you've already finished. Where are you off to so early, son?"

"I'm just finishing up the enclosures at the Russell place." Luke kept his tone neutral, hoping he didn't sound as anxious as he felt to be on his way. His father knew damned well where he went every day and what he did. There wasn't much that went on in the Claiborne family that Gus didn't find out about.

"Sit and have a cup of coffee with me before you go," Gus said. "I hardly see you these days."

"Yes, sir." Luke had too much respect for his father to refuse, and knew if Gus wanted him to sit, there must be a reason. He poured them each a cup of coffee and then leaned back in his chair as if he had all the time in the world.

"Evan told me what you're doing for Jorie," Gus said. "You've been working over there for almost a full week."

Luke gave a dismissive shrug. "I need something to keep me busy until I figure out what I'm going to do with the rest of my life." He tried, and failed, to keep the underlying bitterness out of his voice.

"Volunteering at the fire department isn't enough?"

"Let's just say it's been a pretty quiet summer and the full-time guys have it under control."

"You could apply for a permanent position in the department," Gus said. "Or why not talk to Chief Highwater about a job? You were a military police officer, so you already have the training and the credentials. You'd be a terrific asset to the Last Stand police force."

Luke gave his father a tolerant look. "Even if my hearing loss isn't an issue, I'm not sure I'm cut out for traffic stops and citations."

"You miss the army." Gus said it as a statement, not a question.

"I do, in certain ways."

"You didn't have to get out, son. You could have stayed in."

Luke nodded. "Yup. I could've worked a desk job, or maybe become an instructor at an army base somewhere, but Elsa still would have deployed with a different handler and I would have been reassigned out of the military K9 unit."

"Maybe you should get yourself another dog."

Luke resisted the idea. There wasn't another dog alive

who could replace Elsa. "I'm willing to wait for her to be retired."

"Has there been any improvement in your hearing?"

"What?" Seeing his father's expression, Luke laughed. "Sorry, bad joke. No, I still have almost no hearing in the left ear."

"When do you see the doctor again?"

Luke swirled his coffee and didn't meet his father's eyes. "I don't see much point in going back. Three different specialists agree the damage is permanent."

"Then why don't you wear the hearing aid they gave you? It would improve the quality of what you can hear."

"I can hear fine with my good ear."

"Evan said he couldn't get your attention in the ware-house fire last week." Gus gave him a speculative look. "Said he called your name several times, and you didn't even respond. He's concerned."

"I don't want people to see it and treat me differently." He paused. "If everyone begins raising their voices when they talk to me, I'll go nuts. No thanks."

Luke knew he sounded like a grouch, but he disliked talking about his hearing loss because the truth was, he did miss some of what was said around him. And if there was too much ambient noise, he missed a lot.

"Your hearing loss isn't something to be ashamed of, son. You're a war hero. You and Elsa saved countless lives by locating IEDs before they could injure anyone."

"Thanks, Dad. I'm not ashamed, I'm just—" He didn't know how to explain it to his father, this feeling of having been cast adrift, of no longer knowing where he belonged. He wanted to be back with his unit, conducting patrols with Elsa. When he'd become a K9 handler, his entire life had centered around his dog. He'd gone over the events of that day so many times, but he couldn't see any other outcome than the one he was now living with.

"Look at it this way, son," Gus said. "Would you have done anything different, given the chance?"

Luke stared at his father. He didn't know how, but his dad always seemed to know exactly what he was thinking. "No, I don't believe so."

"Then there's no reason for you to second-guess your actions that day, and I know you do. You saw a child in danger, and you made a split decision. But if you hadn't already been moving away from that IED, you could have been killed. Elsa could have been killed. That child would almost certainly have been killed. So while I know you think you should have done something different, I think you did the only thing you could."

Luke nodded. He'd heard this all before, both from his commanding officer and from the military shrink who'd evaluated him after the incident. He and Elsa had gone into a village in Afghanistan to clear the roads ahead of an infantry unit. Elsa had been walking ahead of him, doing her job, when he'd spotted a child no more than two or three years old, wandering out of an open doorway and into the street. A truck had been accelerating out of an alley, on a direct collision course with the child and Luke had made a split decision. He'd sprinted toward the child and snatched him up at the same time Elsa detected a buried explosive. He'd just had time to call her to his side when the thing detonated, and the force of the blast had sent all three of them careening into the side of the building. The explosion had ruptured Luke's eardrums and caused permanent damage to the bones in his left middle ear. He was just grateful that Elsa and the child hadn't been seriously injured.

"Well, it's all in the past now. As much as I don't like thinking of Elsa working with another handler, at least she's alive. I'm hoping when she retires, I'll be able to adopt her."

"That'll be tough on her current handler," Gus observed. "They'll have the same bond that you two did."

Luke refused to believe that. He'd worked with Elsa from the time she'd been little more than a pup. He'd been her first handler. They'd been inseparable. There was no way another soldier could know Elsa the way he did.

"Possibly, but the policy is that a dog's first handler gets dibs on adoption." There was no way he'd give Elsa up. "If the army offers her to me, I'm taking her. She deserves to spend the rest of her life on a ranch like Riverrun."

"That sounds fine, and it will be good to have another dog on the ranch," Gus said. "Have you spoken with anyone in your unit to see how she's doing?"

"Not recently," Luke said. "I've tried calling my former commander and several of my buddies, but haven't had any luck getting through to them, and no one is returning my calls. The last I heard, she was still deployed in Afghanistan, but her unit should be returning soon."

"Will they let you see her?"

Luke shook his head. "No. It would only confuse her. She'll have bonded with her new handler, and seeing me could complicate that."

"What about the Distinguished Service Medal? Have you heard anything more on that?" Gus asked.

Luke's commanding officer had recommended him for the prestigious award, not only for his years of service as a military police officer, but for his actions on the day of the explosion, when he had rescued that child from the street.

"I did get a call that the award was approved," he said. "I'm just waiting to hear when and where the presentation ceremony will take place."

"Excellent," Gus said. "Congratulations, son. I'm very proud of you, and you should be very proud of yourself. You've done well."

"Thanks, Dad. That means a lot to me." He grinned. "For now, at least, I get to be a full-time cowboy, and I'm looking forward to it."

Gus laughed. "You're a heck of a cowboy, son. I'm happy to have you home."

Luke stood up, anxious to leave. The conversation was veering into territory that made him feel both emotional and helpless. He hated both. "Listen, Dad, I don't want to be rude, but I promised Jorie I'd head over there before she has to leave for the clinic."

Gus waved him off. "Of course, don't let me keep you. Why don't you bring Jorie to the house for dinner on Thursday night? I'm sure Emmaline would like to see her."

"Sure, Dad." Luke didn't want to tell his father yet again

that there was nothing going on between him and Jorie. Hell, he wasn't sure she would come even if he did invite her. She'd be more likely to accept if the invitation came from Emmaline.

When Luke pulled into Jorie's driveway and parked next to her SUV, he saw she hadn't yet gotten new tires. In fact, the car still sported the spare donut tire he'd replaced two days earlier. But as he walked around the mobile home to the rear of her property, he noted with satisfaction that the new enclosures looked sturdy and neat. He and Evan had cut down several trees in the woods behind the trailer and dragged them into the enormous cages to create a realistic environment for the animals. Tree trunks and large limbs crisscrossed the interior, and they had hung a sturdy wooden rope bridge near the top. He moved in for a closer look. Several small hammocks strung from the branches, as well as a series of roped enrichment toys. He grinned at the four raccoons asleep on the bridge, their limbs dangling over the edge, and two more snuggled together in the hammock.

In the second enclosure, there was no sign of the three young foxes, but Luke guessed they were hiding inside the hollowed-out tree trunk that stood in one corner of the cage.

"Hey, I wasn't expecting to see you so early."

Luke turned to see Jorie walking across the grass from the trailer. She wore a pink tank top and a pair of snug blue jeans that emphasized her long legs and extreme slenderness. Her blond hair was loose around her shoulders and Luke knew he was staring, but he couldn't help himself. She smiled at him in a way that made him forget about his earlier glumness. She had two large stainless bowls in her arms, stacked one on top of the other, and he could see the top one was filled with fresh vegetables and fruit.

"Good morning," he said. He felt his mood lighten as she approached him. "Yeah, I wanted to finish up the last bit of work on the older enclosures before it gets too hot to work outside. I hope I didn't wake you up."

Unbidden, he had a mental image of Jorie lying slim and naked and tangled in bedclothes. The vision was so clear and so erotic that he shoved his hands into his front pockets in case his body began to betray him.

"Are you kidding?" she asked, and laughed. "I feel like I've been up for most of the night feeding baby squirrels. I've managed to get by on just a few hours of sleep for years."

"Here," he said, reaching for the bowls. "Let me help you with those."

She let him take the bowls with a grateful smile. "Thanks. This first bowl goes into the enclosure with the raccoons, and this one underneath is for the foxes."

Peering into the bottom bowl, Luke saw it contained some kind of raw meat. "What's this?"

"Duck patty," she said brightly. "I feed the foxes a raw diet, and they're always completely stoked for this meal. But it's expensive, so they don't get it every day. Usually, it's just kibble and apples."

"How expensive is it?" He knew she couldn't have much extra money, not when she was budgeting to save up for new tires, and he didn't know how she managed to keep the rehab clinic operating on just her own salary.

"For feeding all of them? About seven hundred dollars a month." Jorie opened the door to the raccoon enclosure and took the first bowl from him, stepping inside and pulling the wire door closed behind her. "I do get some donations from the community," she said, emptying the contents of the bowl onto a wide, wooden platform on the ground. "But I typically end up paying for most of it myself."

She stood back with the empty bowl, and they watched as the raccoons slowly made their way down from their various perches and waddled over to the food, where they used their tiny hands to eat in a way that was uncannily human.

"Well, that should hold them over until this afternoon," Jorie said, satisfaction in her voice. She stepped out of the enclosure and locked the door. "Want to see the foxes?"

"Sure." Luke just wanted to watch Jorie. He liked how comfortable she was in this environment, and her concern for the animals under her care was evident in everything she did. He handed her the bowl containing the duck patty, and took the empty one from her.

Opening the wire door to the fox enclosure, she stepped inside and Luke closed it behind her. There was a stack of smaller bowls by the entrance. Jorie divided the food between the bowls and then set them away from each other.

"Foxes won't generally fight over something as low value as food, but they really love this stuff so I want to be sure they each get a fair portion," she explained, as she stepped out of the enclosure and carefully locked the door. "Watch."

They stood several feet away and, as they waited expectantly, two small foxes crept out of the hollow tree, their noses pointed in the air as they caught the scent of the duck patty.

"Look how sweet they are," Jorie whispered, leaning closer to Luke. "They were found in the woods behind someone's shed, apparently abandoned. The third one is still afraid to come out when I'm nearby, but they've come a long way since they first arrived."

Jorie's arm pressed against his and, as she leaned toward him, he could smell the light, floral fragrance of her shampoo and soap. He had to resist the urge to dip his head and breathe her in. "When will you release them back into the wild?"

"Pretty soon," she murmured, her eyes on the foxes. "They're almost big enough to survive on their own."

She looked up at Luke and he found himself arrested by the soft expression in her hazel eyes. "Thank you for everything you've done, Luke. You have no idea how much it means to me. Sometimes I feel so overwhelmed that I just want to give up. Then something happens, like you and Evan coming over to build new enclosures, and my faith in humanity is restored."

Luke searched her eyes, seeing the vulnerability there. "Jorie, I'm sure any number of people in Last Stand would be happy to help you. You just need to ask."

She dropped her gaze. "Maybe you're right, but that's where I draw the line. I hate to ask for donations or for volunteers because I'm afraid I'll get a big, fat nothing in return."

Surprised by the admission, Luke put a finger beneath her chin and tipped her face up, forcing her to look at him. "Why would you think that?"

Jorie didn't try to pull away or avoid his gaze. Instead, she looked at him with something like defiance. "I know what the people in town think about my family. About me."

Luke frowned. "Enlighten me."

"They think I come from a low-class family and that I'm probably no better than my floozy mother who ran off and got pregnant." Pulling her chin away from his hand, she continued to look at him. "I always knew I was different than the other kids. Sometimes I would overhear them whispering about me." She gave a self-deprecating huff of laughter. "Trust me when I tell you, it wasn't nice."

Luke felt something tighten in his chest. "Not to sound clichéd, but kids really can be cruel. But you're not your mother, and you had no control over where you lived as a child or who raised you. Nobody is judging you, Jorie, and your life is what you make it." He paused. "I think if you gave them a chance, the people of Last Stand might surprise you."

"What do you mean?"

What did he mean? He'd found himself thinking about Jorie more than he cared to admit during the past week. He told himself it was only because he'd been working at her house, but there was something about her that tugged at him, made him want to know more about her. Made him want to get involved and help her.

"I think you should organize a fundraiser for your animals," he said. "You can't keep paying for everything out of pocket and I'm pretty sure you'd get a good response from the community. People want to help, Jorie."

"I did a fundraiser about six months ago at Honeyman's. You're right; I did get some decent donations, but I hate to keep pestering people for money. They'll get sick of me."

Luke gave her a tolerant look. "Let me guess. Your fundraiser consisted of an empty jar on the counter at the vet clinic, with a sign taped to it that said *Please Donate.*"

"Yes, something like that," Jorie acknowledged, her tone rueful. "Why? What did you have in mind?"

"I think you should have an open house, invite people to come in and see the work you're doing here, get a chance to view the raccoons and foxes and even your stinky little friend, if you think that would be okay."

Jorie gaped at him. "You want me to invite people to come *here*?"

"Sure. Why not?"

Jorie's gaze swept toward the mobile home, and Luke could almost read her thoughts. She was embarrassed about where she lived, and didn't want anyone seeing it. He almost regretted having mentioned a fundraiser since her discomfort was almost palpable.

"Never mind," he said, scrubbing a hand over his face. "I don't have a fucking clue what I'm talking about."

"No, it's a good idea and I promise to think about it, okay? I'll take those back up to the house." Jorie reached for the empty bowls he still carried. But as she took them, one slipped and fell to the ground with a clatter, startling the foxes so that they darted back into the hollow tree.

"Here, let me." Luke bent to pick up the bowl but paused, and then stroked a finger through the dirt and grass at their feet. "I didn't know you smoked."

"I don't." Jorie squatted down next to him to examine what he had found. On the ground outside the enclosures were several fresh cigarette butts. "I have no idea where those came from."

"Must be one of your helpers," Luke said, straightening.

"No, I don't think so." Her voice sounded confused. "None of them are smokers, and even if they were, I wouldn't let them smoke on the property, not this close to the enclosures."

Something in her tone caused Luke to look sharply at her, but then her expression cleared and she gave him a weak smile. "On second thought, maybe you're right. It probably was one of the volunteers. We have someone new and I forget to tell her that I don't allow anyone to smoke on the property."

"Uh-huh." Luke wasn't convinced. "Well, you'll want to remind her not to toss her discarded cigarettes into the grass. With the hot, dry conditions we've been having, it wouldn't take much to spark a fire."

"Of course, I'll let her know." Jorie nodded, but Luke thought her eyes looked clouded, as if her thoughts were miles away. There was something she wasn't telling him. But what? And why?

Chapter Nine

"I'M TELLING YOU, Jessie, someone trespassed on my land last night! To think that some creeper was standing just feet from where I was sleeping!" She shuddered. "How sick is that? And why were they standing by the enclosures? Do you think they wanted to steal the foxes for their fur? Thank goodness I always lock the pen doors at night."

Jorie had worked late at the vet clinic that evening, and had stopped by Rosa's Cantina, which was owned and operated by Jessie's father. She'd intended to just grab takeout, but Jessie had been waiting tables. When she saw Jorie, she told her father she needed a dinner break and insisted Jorie eat with her at one of the outside patio tables. Mexican guitar music played through unseen speakers and over their heads, dozens of colored lights gave the cantina a festive atmosphere. Business was brisk, and most of the tables were occupied.

"You need to report it," Jessie said, setting her fork down. "Tell Chief Highwater. I'm sure he'd agree to have a patrol car make a few extra drives past the house during the night. Do you have any idea who it might have been?"

Jorie had fibbed when she'd told Luke the cigarettes must have been dropped by a new assistant. She didn't have a new assistant, and none of her current volunteers smoked. There was only one person she could think of who smoked cigarettes, and who might have come onto her property uninvited.

Mason Childress.

But why?

Jorie didn't have to think too long or too hard about the reasons he might have for prowling around her home, and each of them was equally terrifying to her. She'd often wondered if he even remembered what happened that night in his truck. He'd been pretty drunk. She almost hoped he didn't, because only a psychopath could be capable of such violence, and then act as if nothing had ever happened. And she really didn't want to think that she'd once been attracted to a psychopath or—even worse—had attracted the attention of one.

She shivered.

Seeing Mason again had completely unsettled her. What reason could he have for returning to Last Stand? After all, his parents barely spent any time here and it seemed Mason had established a life for himself in Austin, working for the family company. Why had he now decided to return?

"I have no idea who it might have been," she said now, in response to Jessie's question. There was no way she wanted anyone to connect her with Mason Childress. She'd never tell anyone what had happened all those years ago. "Maybe I should get a dog."

"Or a dog handler," Jessie murmured and gave a meaningful look over Jorie's shoulder, to the door that led into the restaurant.

Turning, Jorie saw Luke and Evan step onto the patio, followed by Holt, the oldest Claiborne brother. Luke spotted her immediately and he smiled. Jorie felt a surge of pleasure just seeing him. He walked over to their table while his brothers trailed behind him.

"Hey, Jessie." His gaze turned to Jorie and lingered. "Hi there. I didn't expect to see you tonight."

"I was on my way home from work and thought I'd grab some takeout, but Jessie persuaded me to sit down and eat with her, instead. I didn't know you came here to eat. Doesn't Rosa-Maria cook the same food for you at home as the cantina?"

Luke suppressed a grin and his gaze slid to Holt, who was sitting down at a nearby table with Evan. "She does, but she has the night off and Holt had a craving for carne asada. And you know nobody makes it better than Rosa's Cantina."

Jorie risked a quick glance at her friend, but Jessie was watching Holt with a fixed intensity that was almost embarrassing to witness. Beneath the table, Jorie gave her a sharp kick. Startled, she scowled at Jorie and stood up.

"I have to get back to work," she said, and began gathering up her plate and silverware. "Take my advice and report the intruder to Chief Highwater, okay?" With a last, meaningful look at Jorie, she swept from the patio, leaving them alone at the table.

"What the f—what is she talking about?" Luke asked

softly, in a voice low enough that only Jorie heard him. Somehow, that softness was more menacing than if he had shouted. He pulled Jessie's chair out and sat down, then leaned across the table and pinned her with a hard stare. "Tell me."

Jorie's gaze slid to where Holt and Evan sat across the patio. "Your brothers—"

"—have figured out that I'd rather have dinner with you," he finished evenly. "Did someone break into your house, Jorie, or does this have to do with the cigarettes we found this morning?"

"I may have fibbed when I said I had a new assistant," she confessed. "I just didn't want you to make a big deal out of it, because I'm sure it's nothing."

"Do you know who it was?" he asked quietly.

Glancing at him, he seemed relaxed but she somehow knew it was only an act for her benefit. "I have a suspicion, but that's all," she finally said, reluctantly. "But it could have been anyone."

"Or it could have been someone." He paused. "Have you finished eating?"

"Yes."

"Then why don't I follow you back to your place? I'll take a walk around and make sure everything's okay."

"You really don't need to," Jorie protested. "One of my volunteers, Barbara, has been there since this afternoon. She'll only have left about an hour ago, so I'm sure everything is fine."

"I don't mind," he said easily, but there was something

in his tone that made Jorie look sharply at him. He had been a military police officer. Did he know something that she didn't? She couldn't deny she felt safer with him there, a layer of protection between her and whatever might lurk in the darkness. She only wished he could stay.

"Thank you," she finally said, and reached into her purse to withdraw enough money to cover the meal. "I'd appreciate that. Sometimes it feels very isolated out there."

"Why do you stay?"

"Where else would I go? Besides, I have the animals to think of."

"Okay, then." He gave her a brief smile. "I have my truck. I'll follow you."

He stopped by the table where his brothers were sitting and spoke briefly with them before following her out of the cantina and into the parking lot, where his pickup truck was parked.

"I'll be right behind you," he said, with a reassuring smile.

As she drove through town and across the narrow Hickory Creek Bridge, she was acutely aware of the headlights that followed her, and of the man who sat behind the wheel. She had friends in Last Stand, but none of them had ever offered to come out to her property to check on her, or to make sure she felt safe before locking up for the night. Then again, she never dated and hadn't developed any meaningful friendships with the local men. She wasn't unaware of what was said about her; that she was odd and standoffish, preferring the company of her wild animals to real people. Honestly, there were times she agreed with them.

But knowing Luke Claiborne would do this for her made her feel a little special, as if her well-being was important to him. Jorie couldn't recall the last time anyone had cared about her welfare. Her grandmother certainly hadn't, but Jorie never blamed her. They'd done their best, but some people just weren't meant to raise children.

They reached her driveway and Jorie was drawn out of her thoughts by the sight of Barbara's car parked near the trailer. More surprising, all the lights were on in the small home, including the rear floodlight that illuminated the wildlife enclosures. Parking her car next to Barbara's, Jorie turned off the engine and stepped out. Luke parked the truck and came around to stand beside her.

"I thought you said your volunteer left over an hour ago," he said.

"She was supposed to," Jorie said, walking toward the trailer. "I have no idea why Barbara is still here. I hope everything is okay."

Even as she spoke, the front door opened and Barbara stepped outside. A slight woman in her early sixties, she split her time volunteering at the feline rescue and the wildlife rehab center. Now, there was no mistaking the anxiety on the older woman's face.

"Oh, Jorie, I'm so glad you're back!" she exclaimed and hurried down the steps to intercept Jorie in the driveway. "I was just trying to call you when I saw your car. Someone released the animals!"

For a moment, Jorie failed to understand. "What are you

saying?"

"Someone cut the padlocks and opened the doors," Barbara said, her face twisted in a mixture of anger and regret. "I was in the house, feeding the babies and I never heard a thing. I might not even have noticed except that I heard an engine revving. I thought it might be you, but when I didn't see your car, I got nervous." She paused. "I went out back to check on the raccoons, and they were gone. Then I saw the fox enclosure had also been tampered with."

"I'm Luke Claiborne. How long ago did you realize the animals were gone?"

"Less than twenty minutes ago. I was just feeding the baby squirrels when I heard the car engine." She looked apologetically at Jorie. "I thought maybe I could entice the raccoons back with food, but I haven't seen any of them."

Jorie struggled to think. Who would do such a thing? She always kept the pens locked to ensure this sort of thing didn't happen accidentally. The only bright spot was that the older raccoons and the foxes had been at the rehab center for several weeks, and they had a good chance of surviving on their own. But why would anyone deliberately mess with her animals?

"Show me the pens," Luke was saying now. He'd retrieved a powerful flashlight from his pickup truck.

"Did you see anyone?" Jorie asked, as they made their way behind the trailer.

"No. Like I said, I had no idea anyone was here until I heard the car engine revving at the end of the driveway," Barbara said. "I just hope they didn't hurt the animals."

When they reached the enclosures, Luke crouched down and examined the broken padlocks that lay on the ground. The doors to each of the pens was open, and a quick search confirmed that the raccoons and foxes were gone.

"What are you thinking?" Jorie asked, bending down to look at the locks.

"The padlocks were removed with a bolt cutter," Luke said. "This was planned."

"Maybe it was an animal-rights activist, who thought they were doing the right thing by releasing the animals," Jorie suggested hopefully.

"Maybe," Luke acknowledged, but he sounded doubtful. "But that doesn't make it right. There are laws against trespassing and destruction of private property."

"You don't think whoever did this took them, do you?" Barbara asked.

Luke stood up and trained the beam of the flashlight onto the ground as he searched the entire area. "No, I don't think so. There's fresh scat over here by the tree line, probably from one of the raccoons. I'd say they've escaped into the woods."

"They should be okay," Jorie said, more to reassure herself. "They would have been ready for release in another week or so, anyway."

"Should we call the police?" Barbara asked. "I hate to think of you out here alone. What if whoever did this decides to come back?"

"The animals are gone. There wouldn't be any reason to return," Jorie replied. "You should go home, Barbara. I'll file a report in the morning, but there isn't anything more you can do here."

"Are you sure?" Her glance flickered uncertainly to Luke. "I can stay the night, if you'd like."

"I'll be fine, really."

"I can spend the night," Luke interjected. "On the cot, of course, just to be sure nothing else happens."

If Barbara was surprised by Luke's offer, she didn't let it show. "Well, Jorie, if that sounds acceptable to you, then I'll be on my way. I have to say, I'll feel better knowing Luke is here with you."

Jorie was almost too dumbfounded by Luke's words to respond. Her first instinct was to protest, because she absolutely did not want Luke Claiborne to spend the night in her woefully small home. But neither did she want to spend the night by herself, not when the person who had tampered with the enclosures could return. So she forced herself to smile, as if it was no big deal.

"If Luke doesn't mind sleeping on the cot, then he's welcome to stay," she murmured, avoiding Luke's eyes.

They returned to the mobile home and, after Barbara left, the space seemed to shrink in size. Jorie was accustomed to working with one or two other people in the clinic room, and while space was limited, she'd never noticed just how tiny the area actually was. It seemed she couldn't move without brushing up against Luke.

"What can I do to help?" he asked, after watching her methodically check on each of her small patients. He was sitting on the edge of the narrow cot and Taco had made herself comfortable on his lap. Jorie watched as he absently stroked the cat's fur, eliciting a deep, contented purring. The sight of his strong hands gently scratching behind Taco's ears mesmerized her. Jerking her attention away, she swiftly read through the notes that Barbara had left. Jorie almost wished she needed to mix up more formula, or change the bedding in the cages; anything that would delay her having to actually interact with the big man who sat watching her. But Barbara had thought of everything and there was nothing left to be done.

"It looks like Barbara took care of all the feedings, so there really isn't much to do for another few hours," she admitted. She glanced toward the door that led to her private living quarters. She wasn't ashamed of her home; she'd invested time and money into making it more modern, but she knew it didn't come close to Claiborne standards. "If you're interested, I could find a movie to watch."

"That sounds great," Luke said and stood up, gently placing the cat on the floor. "But I don't want to make you uncomfortable, Jorie. I want to stay because I'm concerned about your safety. I don't mind just hanging out here, on the cot. You don't need to entertain me."

His words caused an unfamiliar warmth to bloom in her midsection and, for a moment, she could only stare at him. She'd never been good at expressing her feelings. Sometimes it seemed she'd spent her entire life suppressing her emotions, because she'd learned early on that they made people uncomfortable. Heck, they made *her* uncomfortable. But looking at Luke, she realized she no longer wanted to live in an emotional fortress. She'd been half in love with him for as long as she could remember. If she wanted to let him in—if she wanted to let anyone in—she'd need to begin dismantling the walls she'd built around herself.

"No," she finally said, as her heart thudded hard and her palms grew damp. "I'm happy for you to stay. I *want* you to stay."

Chapter Ten

L UKE HAD SOME idea of what it had cost Jorie to admit that, and he forced himself to appear unaffected. She reminded him of one her little foxes, ready to bolt at the first sign of danger. But inwardly, he was turning cartwheels of delight. He hadn't planned on running into Jorie tonight, but he couldn't deny he was pretty happy with the direction of the evening. He'd thought of little else but her for the past week or so, and he'd been wracking his brain trying to think of a way to be alone with her without spooking her.

"Just tell me where you want me, and I'll stay out of your way," he said.

"I don't mind watching a movie together," Jorie said, with a nervous smile. "If you want to, that is. Unless you have something else you'd rather do."

Her words caused Luke's already vivid imagination to take off, and it was only with effort that he reined in the erotic images. "A movie sounds great," he assured her.

Jorie frowned. "You came to the cantina for dinner, but you never actually had anything to eat. Are you hungry?"

Luke shrugged. "I'm okay. Don't worry about me."

Clearly, she wasn't going to relax until she'd fed him, but

when she opened her refrigerator, he could see the choices were limited.

"I made a peach cobbler yesterday," she offered. "Does that sound good?"

"That sounds perfect," he assured her.

He watched as she dished out two generous helpings of the cobbler and warmed them in the microwave. "Which do you prefer, wine or coffee with your dessert?" she asked. "I have a nice white wine that I picked up the other day, and I've been dying to try it." She looked a little sheepish. "But I always feel a little pathetic drinking alone. In fact, I rarely ever drink for that reason."

Luke grinned. "Far be it from me to let a lady feel pathetic."

She gave him a grateful smile and handed him a slender bottle of wine. Luke examined the label and gave an approving nod. "An Asher Wolf wine, very nice."

"Yes, Emmaline and I went to one of his wine-tasting events," Jorie said, as she handed him two wineglasses. "She's still trying to decide which wine to serve at the wedding."

"That reminds me," Luke said as he poured them both a glass. "How would you like to come for dinner on Thursday night? We try to pull the family together at least once a week, and Thursday has become the night we do that."

Jorie paused. "That sounds like a family-only thing, Luke. Are you sure I'd be welcome?"

Coming to stand beside her, Luke pressed a wineglass into her hand. "It was my father's idea," he said softly. "But even if he hadn't suggested it, I would have."

Jorie turned around so that her back was against the counter. Up close, she was even prettier, her wide hazel eyes an intriguing mixture of green, gold and brown, framed in thick, dark lashes. Her skin was smooth and pale, flawless except for a faint scattering of pale copper-colored freckles across the bridge of her nose. But when his gaze dropped to her mouth, he swallowed hard. Her lips were lush, parted now as her breathing escaped in short, rapid exhales.

"Then thank you. I'd like to come for dinner," she said.

"Good." Luke's attention was still riveted on her mouth, and now he watched as she nervously moistened her lips, the tip of her tongue a pink temptation he couldn't resist. "I really, really want to kiss you, Jorie Russell. Will you let me?"

He heard her breath catch, and he reached between them to carefully take her wineglass from her fingers and place it on the counter beside his own. He was close enough that he could feel her entire body vibrating like a tuning fork. With great care, he cupped her face in his hands, stroking her soft skin with his thumbs. A sigh escaped her, and she closed her eyes. Taking that as assent, Luke bent his head and covered her mouth with his own.

As he'd imagined, her lips were soft and pillowy. She didn't open for him, and he didn't press her, just continued to kiss her with all the restraint he could manage. Except for his hands bracketing her face, he made no other move to touch her. After a moment, he felt her body relax and she kissed him back, tentatively at first and then with more boldness. Luke let her take the lead, but when she cautiously pressed her tongue against his, it was all he could do not to haul her into his arms and kiss her thoroughly, the way he wanted to. She made an incoherent sound of need and deepened the kiss, exploring his mouth with her lips and tongue, until Luke's body grew hard.

He pulled back, breaking the kiss, but keeping her face in his hands. He dragged in an uneven breath. "That was nice," he murmured. "Really nice."

Jorie gave a shaky laugh, hectic color riding high on her cheeks. "I'm sorry. I hope I didn't shock you."

Dipping his head, Luke looked directly into her eyes. "Don't apologize, Jorie. Nothing you can do would ever shock me. I enjoyed every second of that, and while I would gladly do more, I'm not sure you're ready. Just know that I won't do anything you don't want me to."

She nodded, but refused to meet his eyes. "Thank you, I do know that. You're not like—" she broke off and swallowed hard "—other guys."

She had been about to say someone's name, Luke was sure of it. Everything in him wanted to press her for information, but she'd probably ask him to leave. Tamping down his frustration, he gathered up the glasses of wine and the plates of peach cobbler. "How about that movie?" he asked. "Lead the way."

He followed her down the corridor to what must have once been a bedroom, but had since been converted into a cozy living room. A older but comfortable-looking love seat faced a small, flat-screen television balanced on top of an old trunk. Luke placed the wine and the two plates of cobbler down on a rustic coffee table.

"Is that one of Emmaline's works?" he asked, indicating a large painting of abstract poppies over the sofa.

"Yes! Isn't it gorgeous? I made the mistake of telling Emmaline how much I loved it when I saw it at her gallery opening, and she gave it to me." Jorie grimaced. "I feel a tiny bit guilty because I'm sure she could have sold it for a lot of money, but then I look at it and am so glad it's mine!"

"Yeah, she sure does nice work," Luke agreed. "She gave me one of her paintings to hang in the cabin. Dresses the place up a bit."

"You're not staying at the main house?"

"No. I need my space. Don't get me wrong, my family is great, but I've grown used to being on my own. I just can't get used to Rosa-Maria cleaning my room and doing my laundry."

Jorie looked at him in surprise. "She does that? I mean, I know she always did that when we were kids, but she still does everyone's laundry?"

Luke laughed. "Oh, yeah. Well, except for Holt's. He won't let her anywhere near his stuff. She wasn't happy when he drew that line. I honestly think she enjoys looking after my dad and brothers."

"I think you're right," Jorie agreed. "Otherwise why would she have stayed on for so many years?"

Luke slid her a sideways look. He had his own suspicions, but he'd keep those to himself for now. "Why, indeed?"

They sat down on the sofa, and Luke made sure to keep Jorie on his hearing side. She picked up the remote and after some friendly bickering, they agreed to watch a romantic comedy.

"I can't do horror movies or war movies, and I don't watch anything where women are victimized," she explained in apology. "So that pretty much leaves comedy and Disney. Do you mind?"

Luke shrugged. "I hardly ever watch television, so this is a nice treat for me."

Jorie scrolled through the selections and chose a romantic comedy from the free offerings. As the opening credits rolled, Jorie considered him. "So what do you do in the evenings, if you don't watch television?"

Luke blew out a hard breath. "Well, I'm usually helping Holt or Evan on the ranch during the day and by the time I've had supper and settled in for the night, I'm pretty beat. If I'm not up at the house keeping my dad company, I usually just read a book."

Luke wondered how much she knew about the Claiborne family dynamics. She was friends with Emmaline, so he figured she was aware of the facts, like how his father's first wife had died shortly after giving birth to Holt. Two years later, he'd married again and his second wife—Luke's mother—had given birth to him and Evan. But the marriage hadn't lasted and when they were just toddlers, she'd run off with a minor league baseball player, leaving him and Evan with their father. Gus had had the courage to marry a third time, to Emmaline's mother, a native New Yorker. From what Luke understood, nobody was surprised when four years later, she packed up her young daughter and returned to the city. What had surprised most people was the reason she'd left. Gus had had an extramarital affair with a local woman, resulting in the birth of his younger daughter, Callie. He'd refused to marry Callie's mother, but he'd been a good father to Callie.

If the Claiborne sons had a reputation for being commitment-adverse, Luke figured they had good reason.

"Can I ask you a personal question?" he asked. "I know your mother wasn't always reliable, but what about your father?"

Jorie raised her eyebrows and blew out a breath. "Wow. I can't remember the last time anyone asked about him. The last I heard, and that was about ten years ago, he was working on an oil rig somewhere in the Gulf of Mexico. He never acknowledged me, and I've never even considered reaching out to him. Why would I? He made it clear to my mother that he had no interest in being a father."

"And your mother?"

Jorie shook her head. "The last time I saw her was at my grandmother's funeral. She came home for that, but she didn't stay. Maybe it's awful to say, but I think she only showed up because she'd hoped there was some money in it for her." She made a scoffing sound. "But my grandparents didn't have any money. They only had the trailer and the property and they left both to me. When my mom realized I wouldn't sell either, she left again. I haven't seen her since."

"I'm sorry. I shouldn't have asked."

"No, it's fine." Jorie smiled. "I made my peace regarding my family a long time ago. My grandparents weren't easy to live with, and my mother had a rebellious streak. I just hope one day she finds whatever it is she's looking for. I would like for her to be happy. What about your mom? Do you ever see her?"

"Sure, now and then. She lives out on the West Coast and I get out there when I can. Evan and I used to spend a couple of weeks with her each summer, but that ended when we were about nine." He slanted Jorie a rueful smile. "We were pretty rambunctious and we didn't exactly fit in with her posh friends. I think it was a relief to all of us when she opted to fly out here every year, instead, and spend a weekend in town."

"I'm sorry. That must have been hard for you."

"Not really." He shrugged. "We preferred to be at the ranch and Rosa-Maria was always there for us."

"She's an amazing woman. Part of the reason I loved coming to the ranch when I was a kid was because Rosa-Maria always spoiled me." Jorie smiled. "She would always make sure I had enough to eat and would send me home with enough clothes to last me a few months. I grew fast, and my grandmother didn't have the means to buy me much."

They were quiet for several long moments as they watched the movie, but Luke didn't think either of them was really paying any attention. Since coming home, he'd rarely watched any television. When he did, he preferred the closed-captioned feature, but no way would he ask Jorie to turn that on for him. He preferred the illusion that his hearing was perfect.

"What are your long-term plans, now that you're no

longer in the military?" she asked, during a break in the movie.

Luke had avoided this subject as much as possible, mostly because he had no idea what he wanted to do. "I'm not sure, to be honest. I loved being a military police officer, and I really enjoyed working with Elsa."

"Couldn't you be a K9 officer for a civilian police force?"

"Well, here's the thing," he admitted. "I've lost most of the hearing in my left ear."

Jorie nodded. "That makes sense."

Luke felt his eyebrows go up. "How so?"

"Sometimes I say things to you and you don't seem to hear me. Then I began noticing how you always walk on one side of me and never the other, and how you tip your head when I talk, as if you're trying to hear me better." She shrugged. "I figured you had some hearing loss. It's not uncommon. My grandfather was a helicopter mechanic for most of his life and he was very hard of hearing, so I know the symptoms."

Luke sat back, surprised. He'd been so sure he'd kept his hearing loss under wraps, but apparently he hadn't done such a great job.

"Would you like me to turn on the subtitles?" Jorie asked, as if she could read his mind.

Luke's automatic response was to adamantly insist he had no trouble hearing. But Jorie had already guessed his secret and she didn't seem the least bit fazed by the knowledge.

"Sure," he said, and watched as she used the remote to select the closed-captioned feature.

"You could consider a hearing aid," Jorie said, glancing at him. "They've come a long way with the technology. Nobody would ever need to know you were wearing one. They're tiny and even wireless now." Luke gave a non-committal grunt, but Jorie only laughed. "Okay, maybe not."

Picking up a plate of peach cobbler, she handed it to him before taking her wineglass and scooting close enough that her arm pressed against his. As he tucked into the sweet dessert and with Jorie's warmth beside him, he found his hearing loss no longer seemed as big of an issue as he'd once believed.

THE ROMANTIC COMEDY had been the perfect choice, Jorie decided, as the end credits rolled across the screen. Sweet, without being too sappy, and funny without being slapstick. He probably wouldn't admit it, but she suspected Luke had enjoyed it just as much as she had. He hadn't made another move on her since the kiss they'd shared in the kitchen. But Jorie had thought of little else during the movie, acutely conscious of his big, warm frame beside her. She'd been fascinated by the size and shape of his hands, recalling how gentle they had been as they'd bracketed her face. She'd replayed that kiss again and again in her mind during the movie, recalling the warm, firm pressure of Luke's mouth against her own. His thumbs had stroked her cheeks, and only when she'd found herself responding, had he ended the kiss.

She'd actually been disappointed.

She hadn't immediately recognized the sweet throbbing sensation at her center for what it had been: *desire.* But the knowledge that Luke could actually make her want him had been a heady realization. Her brain knew she wanted him, but she hadn't been certain her body would feel the same way. She sighed happily and leaned forward to scoop up their dishes at the same time Luke did. Their hands brushed, and they nearly bonked heads. Jorie immediately snatched her hand back.

"Whoops, sorry," she said, embarrassed. "I was just going to bring the dishes into the kitchen."

"That's okay, I can do it," Luke said, but he made no move to collect the plates and glasses. Instead, he turned toward her. "Jorie . . .?"

He was so close that she could see the individual stubbles of new beard growth on his jaw, and his eyes seemed impossibly dark. A muscle worked in one lean cheek, and he was staring at her mouth with such intensity that Jorie would have to be blind not to know what he wanted.

"You want to kiss me again," she said, her voice little more than a whisper. Her body had already begun to thrum with the same excitement she'd felt earlier. Her heart rate accelerated, and something heavy and sweet unfurled in her center, spreading languorously through her limbs until she felt as if she might melt into a puddle of sugary syrup right there on the sofa.

"Hell, yes, I want to kiss you," Luke said, his voice deep

and gravelly. "I've wanted to since the day I saw you behind the warehouse."

Jorie suppressed a laugh of surprise. "You did? But you seemed so . . . so furious when you found me trying to sneak in."

"Only because it would have been a shame to see someone as pretty as you die unnecessarily."

"Oh!"

Before she could tell him that she had no intention of doing anything so silly, he bent his head and nuzzled the side of her neck, his breath warm against her skin. Jorie twisted to find his mouth. Unlike their earlier kiss, he didn't hold back. He slid one big hand beneath her hair to cup the back of her head, and kissed her long and deep, with a hunger that left her weak and trembling. When he finally pulled away, Jorie realized she was clinging to him, her hands curled around his forearms.

"You don't have to stop," she said, her voice a little ragged.

Luke made a sound that was part laugh, part groan and tipped his forehead to hers. "Oh, yeah, I do. Because if we don't stop, darlin', I'm going to want to do other things which you might not be ready for. And even if you are, it's too soon, and you'll have regrets afterward."

Privately, Jorie disagreed. She couldn't imagine ever having regrets about getting involved with Luke. She didn't think any other man could have elicited the same response. But kissing wasn't the same as having sex, and the jury was still out on how she might handle *that*. So she nodded and reluctantly put some space between them. "Okay. I should probably feed the animals and then get to bed." She hesitated. "Are you going home?"

Luke stood up. "I'll help you with the feedings, if you'd like, and then I'll crash on the cot. Just for tonight. I doubt whoever cut the locks on the enclosures is going to come back, but I'd feel better staying. If you don't mind."

"No! Of course I don't mind."

She was actually relieved he still wanted to stay. She hadn't let herself think too much about who might have tampered with the enclosures, but as long as Luke was here with her, she didn't need to.

She was safe with Luke.

She'd file a report in the morning, and then shop for a security system for the property, which meant she'd need to work extra hours at the vet clinic, or delay payment on some of her bills. Pushing the dismal thoughts aside, she followed him as he carried their dishes into the kitchen, and then spent the next hour showing Luke how to mix the various formulas for the baby squirrels, the skunk, and the other small animals she cared for.

"Well, that should do it," she said, when they'd finished. "They'll be fine until morning."

"I'm amazed by what you do here," Luke said. He'd been holding a possum that had been found injured on a roadside more than a month earlier. "When will you release this little guy?"

"I'm actually going to keep *her* here, with me," Jorie said, stepping close to Luke and taking the little, gray furry creature from him. "The vet thinks she was hit by a car. She suffered some nerve damage and can't use her tail. For a possum, that's imperative for survival. But they're very sweet, sociable creatures and they can make wonderful pets."

She underscored her statement by pressing her face into the possum's fur and nuzzling gently.

Luke groaned. "A feral cat, a skunk, and now a possum. Why am I not surprised?"

Jorie smiled and placed the critter back into its cage. "They just want the same things we want."

"And what's that?" Luke arched an eyebrow and his mouth quirked, but Jorie thought his attention sharpened on her, as if her response really interested him.

"We all want a safe place to live, good food, and someone to love us." She tipped her chin up and met his gaze squarely, daring him to mock her. But to her surprise, there was nothing mocking in his expression.

"Maybe you're right," he said. "I'll stay up for a bit. You should go to bed."

"Will you be here in the morning?"

"Don't worry. I'll head out early," he said. "You won't even know I'm here."

He was wrong. She probably wouldn't sleep a wink knowing he was on the cot, a short walk from her own bedroom. Surprisingly, the thought didn't concern her. She felt safe with Luke.

"I'm not worried," she said, "so you don't need to rush out on my account."

Luke chuckled. "Oh, yeah, sweetheart, I do. I really do."

Later that night, lying in her bed and knowing he was just twenty feet away, she replayed the events of the evening. She didn't dare hope that Luke might be starting to have feelings for her. But he had invited her to have dinner with his family. Even if the invitation had been his father's idea, Luke didn't have to agree. But he had, and now Jorie found herself dreaming about things she'd previously thought impossible.

She'd spent a lot of time on the ranch as a child, when she and Emmaline had been friends. And when Emma had returned to New York City for the school year, Jorie had cultivated a friendship with Emma's younger sister, Callie. She would have done anything to spend more time at Riverrun Ranch and escape her own unhappy home life. She'd loved everything about the Claiborne family back then, including Luke.

She still did.

Chapter Eleven

T HERE WAS NO sign of Luke when Jorie woke up the following morning. The blanket and sheets were neatly folded at the foot of the cot. Jorie smoothed a hand over the pillow he had slept on, imagining him there. She didn't have time to fantasize, however, as Barbara arrived to perform the morning feedings.

"No sign of the raccoons?" she asked, as she and Jorie prepared formula and kibble.

Jorie peered through the window toward the enclosures. "No, I think they're really gone."

"Did Luke have any thoughts on who might have cut the locks?" Barbara asked.

Jorie paused in the act of slicing an apple, and then resumed with slightly more force than was necessary. She had her own suspicions, but she wasn't ready to begin throwing accusations around, especially when she knew there would be very few people who would believe her.

"I don't think so, or at least he isn't saying. I'm hoping it was just some local kids playing a prank."

"I'm sure that's what it was," Barbara said soothingly. "Last Stand is a safe town. Chief Highwater sees to that."

Jorie knew she was right, but she still couldn't shake the feeling that Mason Childress had something to do with releasing the animals. But she couldn't imagine why he would do such a thing, unless he deliberately wanted to upset her.

"Well, I should get going," she said, when the animals had been fed. "I want to stop by Matt's garage before I start my shift at the clinic, and talk to him about some new tires for the car. Are you all set here?"

"Absolutely. I'll be here until noon, and I'll set everything up for the afternoon feedings."

"Perfect, thank you!"

Jorie arrived at Matt's garage shortly after they opened, but the small office was empty. She wrinkled her nose at the smell of oil and exhaust, and peered into the garage where two cars were up on hydraulic lifts. She could hear masculine voices from somewhere behind the cars, but she couldn't see anyone. She tapped the bell on the counter and waited. After a moment, a girl stepped into the office. She looked to be about eighteen years old. Her short, dark hair sported two bright pink streaks on one side, and she wore a black hoodie, jeans, and work boots, even though the temperatures were already beginning to climb into the nineties.

"Can I help you?" she asked in a tone that said clearly she had no desire to help anyone.

"I'm Jorie Russell. I'm here to see Matt about some tires," she said, straining to peer into the garage behind the girl. "Is he here?"

"No. He ran out to pick up some parts. I don't know

when he'll be back."

Jorie tamped down her rising frustration. "Okay, well, I need new tires. I was in here earlier this week and Matt told me to bring the car back when I was ready."

"Do you want me to have him call you?"

"Sure." Jorie wrote down her name and number on the pad of paper the girl slid across the counter. "I'm working until five o'clock, but I can bring the car in after that."

The girl glanced at the paper, and Jorie watched as her expression tightened. "You're Jorie Russell? From out on Hickory Creek Road?"

"Yes. Why? Have we met?"

"No, but I remember your grandmother threatened to shoot my dog when I was little."

"Oh! Do you live nearby?"

The girl shrugged. "About a mile down the road."

"Ah," Jorie said. "Well, I'm sorry about that. My grandmother wasn't much of an animal lover, I'm afraid. She didn't want anyone on her property, and that included four-legged visitors. Sometimes, I'm not even sure she wanted me there, so don't take it personally."

But if Jorie thought the last comment would elicit a smile, she was wrong. The girl's expression never changed. Most of the properties on Hickory Creek Road were set back from the street, obscured by trees and overgrowth. Jorie wasn't acquainted with many of the neighbors, but she did know the McGuire family lived nearby.

"Are you Matt's sister, by any chance?" she asked.

"Yeah, why?"

Jorie shook her head. "No reason. It's just nice to finally meet you. We've been neighbors probably since you were born. What's your name?"

"Iris."

"That's a pretty name. Well, thanks for your help, Iris. Please tell Matt I can come by around five, if that works."

"Sure." Iris paused. "You're the one who keeps all those animals at your place, right?"

Jorie smiled. "I do, yes. You're more than welcome to come over and see them, if you're interested. I have a lot of babies at the moment and they're awfully sweet."

"Thanks, but I'm pretty busy." Iris pushed her hands into her front pockets and kicked at the concrete floor with her booted foot. "I mean, maybe I could."

Jorie nodded. "Okay, good. I work at home on Monday and Wednesday each week, so feel free to stop by."

She left the garage, shaking her head. If she didn't know better, she'd think she'd done something to offend the girl. But she also recalled how painfully shy she had been at the same age, and decided she wouldn't take it personally. And Iris had seemed interested in coming over to see the animals. Her feigned disinterest didn't fool Jorie. As she climbed into her car and drove over to the Honeyman Veterinary Clinic, she found herself smiling. Caring for animals had provided her with both a purpose and a direction in her life. Maybe it could do the same for Iris McGuire.

LUKE FOUND HIMSELF feeling out of sorts, knowing Jorie was coming to the ranch for dinner with his family. No matter how many times he told himself it was no big deal—they frequently had dinner guests at the ranch—he acknowledged this was different. He wasn't buying his father's flimsy excuse that he'd invited Jorie because Emmaline might like to see her. Emmaline and Jorie saw each other frequently, so the only conclusion he could draw was that his father was somehow trying to play matchmaker.

"Wow, you clean up well," came a teasing voice from the doorway of his bedroom at the foreman's cabin.

Whirling from the mirror where he'd been buttoning his shirt, he saw his sister, Emmaline, lounging against the doorframe with a grin on her face. Of all the Claiborne siblings, he and Emmaline looked the most alike, with their matching black hair and dark eyes. But Emmaline had been raised in New York City by her mother, and despite having moved back to Last Stand the previous year, she hadn't been able to shed her smart-mouthed, East-Coast attitude.

"Don't people knock where you come from or does everyone just barge in, uninvited?" he replied. But the swift hug he gave her took any sting out of his words.

"I did knock," Emmaline argued, pulling away. "But you must have been so entranced by your own dashing good looks that you didn't hear me."

Luke grunted. He missed more than he cared to admit. Realizing he hadn't heard her knocking was a little disconcerting. "What brings you here? Cort sick of you already and you need someone to kick his ass?"

"*No.*" She perched herself on the edge of his bed. "I just realized that since you've been home, I haven't seen much of you. I was walking past the cabin and I heard you singing."

"I was singing?" He hadn't been aware.

Emmaline smiled. "You were."

Luke frowned. "I can't imagine why."

"Oh, I can," she said, giving him a knowing smile. "And I just want to say I approve. Jorie is a very sweet person. Maybe she'll help soften your rough edges."

"Jesus, why does everyone think we're involved?" Luke frowned. "Dad was the one who invited her to dinner. This invitation had nothing to do with me."

"Uh-huh." She pushed herself off the bed and smoothed the skirt of her sundress. "All I can say is you'd better be nice to her, Luke Claiborne. Jorie is a good friend and I'd hate to see you break her heart. She's had enough heartache in her life."

Luke stilled in the process of putting his wallet into his back pocket. "What do you mean? Did some guy do a number on her?"

He half expected Emmaline to deny that's what she meant, but instead her face grew serious. "Maybe you should ask Evan. Or Callie. I wasn't there, so it's just hearsay."

Something inside Luke coiled tight and then released, like a spring-loaded trigger. "What happened?"

"You know what? Forget I said that. I should never have opened my mouth. If Jorie finds out, she'll never speak to me again."

"Well, you did open your mouth," Luke said, growing

more annoyed by the second as his imagination took off. "So spit it out. What happened?"

Emmaline blew out a hard breath. "I don't know, exactly. Callie told me a story about a house party on the other side of town, back when she and Jorie were in high school."

"Go on," Luke said grimly, as she paused.

"Some college guy was there, hitting on Jorie, but he seemed nice and everyone knew him so she figured it wasn't a big deal. But at some point, Jorie just sort of . . . vanished. It was getting late, and Callie said she couldn't find her, and then Evan was there, dragging her out of the house and into the truck. Callie said she'd never seen him so pissed off. Jorie was already there in the front seat, all curled up in a ball. She was crying and her nose was bleeding." Emmaline's expression turned regretful. "That's all I know."

"You didn't ask Jorie what happened?"

"Yes, of course I *tried*. When Callie told me what happened, I asked Jorie about it but she said she had no idea what I was talking about." She frowned. "Evan never talked to you about that night?"

"No." During the summer in question, Luke had already enlisted in the army. While he and Evan had spoken occasionally on the phone in those days, that particular topic had never come up. "Who was the guy hitting on her?"

"Mason Childress, I think."

Luke nodded, even as something cold and ruthless unleashed itself from deep inside him. "I am going to fucking take him apart. By the time I'm finished with him, there won't be enough money in the world to put him back together."

Emmaline's eyes widened in alarm. "Luke, no! You can't go after the guy. I'm not even one hundred percent certain it was him."

"I am."

"But we don't know for sure that anything happened. You can't just go beating people up! And anyway, it was a long time ago, at least eight or nine years."

"Doesn't matter."

"You can't say anything! Promise me you won't breathe a word of what I just told you. Jorie would be so furious with me for telling you, and I guarantee she would never speak to you again. Is that what you want?"

Luke scrubbed both hands over his face. "No, of course not."

"Then just leave it alone, okay? If she wants you to know, she'll tell you. But in case you haven't noticed, trust isn't one of her strong suits."

"Yeah, I noticed," he said grimly, and blew out a hard breath. Everything in him wanted to hunt the bastard down and smash every bone in his body. If Mason Childress had hurt Jorie, he didn't care how much time had passed. He wouldn't get away with it. At some point, he'd make sure the son of a bitch paid. "Don't worry," he said to Emmaline. "I won't say anything to Jorie."

Emmaline studied him for a moment and then, apparently satisfied with what she saw on his face, she nodded. "Okay. Well, we should probably head up to the house before Cort sends out a search party."

Luke slung an arm around her shoulders and pulled her close, before pressing a brief kiss against her hair. "Thanks for telling me. It's nice to have you back in Last Stand, and I like Cort. He's a stand-up guy."

Emmaline smiled at him. "He's the best there is. Besides the Claiborne men, of course."

They left the cabin and Luke pulled the door closed behind him before they started walking toward the main house. He couldn't stop thinking about what Emmaline had told him. Nine years ago, he'd been training to become a military police officer. Jorie couldn't have been more than seventeen at the time. The thought of anyone physically harming her made his hands curl into fists. If someone *had* hurt her, he was going to make that person pay.

But first, he needed to talk to Evan.

They reached the front steps of the wide, wraparound porch at the same time Jorie's car came down the driveway and stopped in front of the house. Luke pushed his hands into his pockets as Jorie and then Jessie stepped out of the vehicle, and came forward to greet Emmaline.

"Thank you for inviting me," Jessie said, smiling. "It'll be like old times."

"Well, we couldn't invite Jorie and not invite you too. I'm so glad you could make it," Emmaline said. She gave her friend a conspiratorial wink. "And I'm sure someone else will be happy to see you too."

Luke watched with interest as color swept into Jessie's face before she gave Emmaline a swift, warning look. Who was Emmaline talking about? Evan? It seemed all the girls had a thing for Evan, but he'd never indicated any interest in their housekeeper's pretty granddaughter. Then again, Evan had commitment issues. He'd had plenty of girlfriends, but as far as Luke knew he'd never been serious about any of them.

Now he looked at Jorie, who was watching him with an appealing mixture of shyness and pleasure. She looked nice in a pale-blue sundress that cinched in at her waist. She'd left her blond hair loose around her shoulders and Luke wondered if the wheaten strands would feel as silky as they looked.

"Hey, Luke," she said by way of greeting. "I have something in the back of the car. Would you mind getting it for me?"

"That depends. Is it going to spray me or bite me?"

Jorie laughed. "No, you're safe."

Luke wasn't so sure about that. Seeing Jorie made him feel a bit unbalanced, both physically and emotionally. He wanted badly to greet her with a hug or, better yet, a kiss. But he wasn't sure she would welcome either and he wasn't ready to make such a public display of affection.

As he retrieved a tote bag that contained wine and a bouquet of cut flowers, he realized he'd only rarely heard Jorie laugh. He'd need to do something about that, because he liked the sound of her laughter. He followed the women into the house and through to the back terrace, where Rosa-Maria had set a table for nine. The Pedernales River curved behind the property, slow and lazy this time of year. The sun was already beginning to sink behind the trees, and the fairy lights that had been hung overhead gave the terrace a festive air. Soft music played through unseen speakers, and a small bar had been set up in one corner, but nobody was there to enjoy it.

"Where is everyone?" Luke asked.

"Your father and brothers are in his study," Rosa-Maria said.

Luke frowned. Gus didn't typically invite people into his study unless he had serious business to discuss. "Should I go join them? Am I missing something?"

"No, no," Rosa-Marie said hastily. "I will let them know you are here."

Luke arched an eyebrow, noting her near panic. "Okay. Thanks."

The housekeeper hurried down the hallway toward his father's office. If Luke didn't know better, he'd think *he* was the reason for the clandestine meeting. Several moments later, his brothers and father appeared.

"What's going on?" he asked with a grin. "Private family meeting? Planning to cut me out of the inheritance?"

He'd meant it as a joke but to his astonishment, Holt and Evan shared a look that could only be described as guilty.

Interesting.

Luke made a mental note to question his brothers about the meeting, once dinner was over. They were definitely up to something, and he intended to find out what.

"Ah," Gus said to the ladies as he stepped onto the patio. "Some beauty to grace our table. How are you, Jorie?"

"Thank you so much for having me, Mr. Claiborne," she said, as he kissed her cheek. "This patio brings back a lot of happy memories for me."

"I'm happy to see you. And Jessie!" He gave Jessie a hug, then put an arm around her shoulders and led her toward Evan and Holt. "We don't see enough of you around here anymore. Is the cantina keeping you busy?"

"It is, yes," Jessie confirmed. "But I was happy to get away for tonight. This is a real treat for me."

"No," Gus protested "This is a real treat for us. Isn't it, boys?"

Evan nodded and made an appropriate comment, while Holt turned away to make himself a drink at the bar. Jessie's gaze clung to him, and for a moment, Luke saw something in her expression that made him feel like a voyeur. *So that's how it was.* Not Evan. Jessie had a thing for his brother, Holt.

Even more curious was the way Holt seemed to deliberately ignore her.

"If you don't mind," Jessie said to Gus, "I'll just pop into the kitchen and see if my *abuela* needs any help."

"I'll come with you," Jorie offered. "I brought some wine, and the flowers need to be put into a vase."

After they had disappeared into the house, Luke pulled Evan aside. "Hey, bro, mind if we have a private word?"

Evan looked sharply at him. "Sure. Something wrong?"

"I don't know, but you're going to help me decide. I'd appreciate it if we did this quick, before Jorie returns."

Evan's expression turned serious. "Yeah, sure. If it's what

I think, I probably should have said something before now."

They retreated to the far side of the terrace, where they wouldn't be overheard. As Luke listened to Evan, it took everything he had to remain outwardly calm. The more Evan talked, the colder he felt inside. He kept his head down and one eye on the door to the kitchen in case Jorie came back. When Evan finished, he clapped Luke on the shoulder.

"She's fine, bro. I know what you're thinking, but trust me, you don't want to go after Mason Childress. You lay a finger on him, and he'll own our ranch. It's been nine years. Let it go."

Luke nodded. "Yeah. Thanks for telling me, Evan."

"Who else is joining us for dinner?" Emmaline asked, indicating the nine place settings, and distracting them from their discussion. "We're only eight."

"Ah, yes," Gus said. "I invited Rosa-Maria to join us. Since Jessie is here, it didn't seem right not to include her."

"Well, she is almost family." Luke forced himself to smile. "How many years has she been with you, Dad? Twenty-five?"

"Yes, just about." Gus's shrewd blue eyes rested on Luke for a moment, as if he suspected there was more to the casual question. "She's been a good employee. I don't know what I would do without her."

"Well, let's hope you never need to find out," Evan said. "Just don't let her hear you say that. I'm pretty sure Rosa-Maria would be here every day, even if you weren't paying her. But if she thinks you only see her as an employee, you'll be washing your own skivvies in the future."

"Worse," Holt added, twirling his drink, "we'd all have to eat our own cooking."

"Point taken," Gus said with a grin.

"What point is that?" Jessie stepped back onto the terrace, carrying a vase of flowers, followed by Jorie and Rosa-Maria. Each of them carried a bowl or platter of food, and they set everything down on the table.

"We were just saying that nobody cooks like Rosa-Maria." Gus smiled warmly at the older woman. "We're very lucky to have you."

Rosa-Maria smiled with pleasure. "Thank you, *señor*. Jessie, would you help me carry in the remaining dishes?"

"Why don't you let the men do that," Luke said, pulling a chair out for her. "You and the ladies sit down."

"Oh!" Rosa-Maria beamed at him. "Thank you!"

He deliberately sat her at Gus's right side, and then ensured his own seat was next to Jorie's. Dinner was a cheerful event, and Luke couldn't recall the last time he'd enjoyed anything as much as he did that meal, with Jorie laughing by his side. Evan kept everyone entertained with stories about growing up on the ranch, and even Rosa-Maria got into the spirit of the evening, regaling them all with tales about the mischief they'd gotten into as children. But Luke couldn't prevent his gaze from lingering on Jorie's profile, imagining her as a shy teenager. His protective instincts were fully roused, and he promised himself nobody would ever hurt her again.

They sat and talked until the sun vanished over the horizon, and darkness surrounded the ranch. The twinkle lights on the terrace cocooned them in a soft glow. More than once, Luke caught his father watching Rosa-Maria, his blue eyes warm with affection. Gus might want them to think Rosa-Maria was only an employee, but Luke suspected that for his father, she was much more.

At her grandmother's urging, Jessie darted into the kitchen and returned with a decadent dessert that she placed in the middle of the table amidst much groaning.

"I can't eat another bite," Jorie protested, placing one hand over her flat midriff. "I'm completely full!"

Evan gave her a critical look. "C'mon, Jorie, you could use a few extra pounds. Don't make us enjoy this by ourselves."

Luke bristled at the way he was assessing Jorie's shape. He put an arm around her shoulders. "She says she's had enough, and I think she looks great just the way she is."

Evan winked at Jorie and put his hands up in surrender. "I agree, bro, and I wouldn't dream of forcing anyone to eat something as delicious as Rosa-Maria's Mexican chocolate cake, not when it means there will be more for me!"

"Who wants a slice?" Emmaline asked and stood up to cut into the cake.

As she did so, both Luke and Evan's phones began to ding with text message notifications. Evan gave Luke a meaningful look as they both drew their phones out and read them.

"There's a fire out on Hickory Creek Road," Evan said, pushing his chair back. "Gotta go. Sorry."

"Out on Hickory Creek Road?" Jorie repeated, her expression alarmed. "Where on Hickory Creek Road?"

Luke stood up. "It's your place, Jorie," he said, his voice grim. "There's a fire at your place."

Chapter Twelve

DESSERT WAS FORGOTTEN as everyone scrambled from the table.

"Jorie, leave your car here," Luke instructed. "You can ride over with Cort and Emmaline. Evan and I will go now. Don't park near the property in case the emergency vehicles need access, and if there's any sign of flames, *stay back*!"

"Luke, the animals!" Jorie's voice shook, and she found herself consumed with a fear she couldn't seem to control. Even her hands were trembling.

Luke paused. "We'll do everything we can, but I am dead serious, Jorie. If there is any sign of fire, you are not to go into that fu—that house. Agreed?"

His expression was so serious that Jorie found herself nodding. "Just save them, Luke, please. Taco and her kittens have already been through one fire, they can't do this again. *Hurry.*"

At almost the same instant, they heard the distant wail of a fire engine.

"I gotta go," Luke said, and then took her by the arms and hauled her close to press a brief, hard kiss against her mouth. "Try not to worry."

"Jorie and Jessie, you come with us," Cort said, after Luke and Evan had dashed out the door. "My truck is parked out front."

"Dad and I will follow in my truck," Holt said.

Even with the surrounding chaos, Jorie paused and looked at Rosa-Maria. "Thank you for dinner, Rosa-Maria, it was lovely. I'm so sorry to run out like this."

Rosa-Maria pulled her into a swift hug. "No, you don't worry about any of that now. Just go and take care of your animals. And listen to Luke! He will keep you safe."

"Thank you, *Abuela*," Jessie said, and kissed her grandmother before they hurried out to the driveway and climbed into the pickup trucks.

To Jorie, the drive to the Hickory Creek Bridge seemed to take forever, although it couldn't have been more than ten minutes. The road was closed on the other side, and they were delayed for an additional fifteen minutes until they were given the all clear to proceed. As they drove toward Jorie's property, they were forced to pull over to allow an ambulance to race past them in the opposite direction, its siren wailing.

"I hope nobody was hurt," Emmaline murmured, turning in her seat to watch the ambulance as it sped away.

Jorie could see the flashing of the emergency lights before they reached her driveway. There were two police cruisers in the street, and a firetruck parked at the end of the driveway. As they drew closer, a police officer stepped into the road and raised his hand, stopping them. Cort rolled down his window.

"I have the homeowner, Jorie Russell, with me. What happened?"

The officer peered through the window to where Jorie and Jessie sat anxiously in the back seat of the cab with the window open. "Ma'am," he said, touching the brim of his hat. "Looks like the home is a complete loss. There's a propane tank in the back that they're working to stabilize, so I can't let you onto the property yet."

"No," Jorie breathed, and promptly burst into tears. All she could think about were the small souls that had depended on her for their safety—for their very survival, and she had failed them. She thought of sweet little Taco and her babies, and cried even harder.

Emmaline reached over from the front seat and squeezed her hand, her face twisted in sympathy. "I'm so sorry, Jorie."

"Shh, it's okay," Jessie said, putting her arms around Jorie and hugging her tight. "We'll figure this out, please don't cry."

"Do they know what caused the fire?" Cort asked the police officer.

"No, but there will be an investigation. We sent a victim to the hospital less than five minutes ago," the officer said. "First-degree burns, but I don't have any additional information."

"A victim?" Jorie straightened and swiped at her eyes. "One of the firefighters?"

"No, ma'am," the officer replied. "A Good Samaritan, maybe, injured trying to rescue the animals inside the trailer."

Jorie gasped. "Do you know who it is?"

"Sorry, no." He indicated the side of the road. "You can park along here, but please keep your distance from the trailer, as this is still an active fire scene."

Cort parked the truck, and Gus and Holt pulled in behind them. Cort had barely turned off the engine before Jorie was jumping out.

"Whoa, Jorie, hold up," Cort said. "Why don't you let me go ahead and take a look, hmm?"

"I think that's a good idea," Jessie said, catching Jorie's hand and preventing her from running ahead to the driveway. "Once you see something, you can never unsee it. Look, there's Luke."

He appeared at the end of the driveway and, spotting Jorie, began striding toward her. In his turnout coat and helmet, he was barely recognizable, but Jorie would have known him anywhere, and she'd never been so thankful for his presence.

"Luke!" She ran toward him and would have flung herself at him, but he caught her by the arms and held her away from him.

"You don't want to do that, sweetheart," he said. "I'm pretty dirty."

Only then did she notice he was streaked with soot and dirt, and rivulets of muddy water ran down the front of his jacket. She didn't care, but Luke held her firmly away.

"How bad is it?" she asked, her voice fearful.

"I'm not going to lie to you," he said, his voice grim. "It's bad. Looks like the fire started near the enclosures and spread to the house. The mobile home is a complete loss, Jorie. I'm so sorry."

Jorie covered her mouth with her hands as she stared at him, aghast. "And the animals?"

To her utter astonishment, Luke smiled at her. "All accounted for and safe. At least as far as I can tell, but I don't remember every critter you had in there."

"Are you serious? They're safe?"

Luke nodded. "Yes, I promise."

"Oh, Luke, *thank you!*" Uncaring of the soot and mud that coated his jacket, she flung her arms around his neck and gave him a fierce hug, kissing his lean cheek as he gave a bark of surprised laughter and gently disentangled himself.

"Is that true?" Jessie asked. Her smile was tentative and hopeful.

"Yeah, it's true," Luke assured her. "You can come down and see for yourself. We've tried to keep the animals warm and away from the worst of the activity, but they're pretty stressed, and they'll need a new place to rehabilitate."

"Well, that's no problem," Holt said, coming to stand beside Luke. "We can bring them back to Riverrun and put them in the breeding barn. It's climate controlled and dry, and there's plenty of space. They can stay there until Jorie figures out what to do next."

Luke nodded in agreement. "Great idea. I'll ask the guys to load the cages into the trucks."

"Jorie, you'll stay with us at Riverrun as long as you need to," Gus said. "We have plenty of room and I know Rosa-Maria will welcome having another woman in the house.

Meanwhile, I'll call Miles Honeyman and have him send over whatever supplies and food you need for the animals."

Jorie stared at them, too overwhelmed by gratitude to find her voice. She'd thought the worst had happened, and that the animals she'd tried so hard to rescue had died. But they had survived, and now these people were offering to help ensure they continued to thrive. They owed her nothing, and yet they were willing to open their home to her and her wildlife.

"I—I don't know what to say," she said, as new tears threatened to surface.

Emmaline put an arm around her shoulders. "You don't have to say anything. This is what friends do for each other, right? C'mon, let's go get them."

Luke led them down the long driveway, and even surrounded as she was by Jessie, Emmaline and the Claiborne men, Jorie felt her heart plummet into her shoes when she saw the devastation the fire had left behind. A firetruck had pulled close to the trailer and continued to douse the structure with water. Smoke and steam filled the air, and the emergency lights gave the scene an eerie, otherworldly feel. The roof of the mobile home was intact, but large, burned out holes in the walls revealed charred studs and insulation. Jorie could see that nothing of the interior had survived the blaze. Firefighters worked the perimeter of the property, putting out hot spots and ensuring there was no chance for the fire to reignite.

"Where are they?" she asked, looking away from the wreckage of what had once been her home.

"Over here." Luke led her to an area away from the fire-truck and the remains of the mobile home. Stacked in neat rows on top of each other were a dozen or more crates and cages. Someone had covered them with a tarp, and when Jorie cautiously lifted one edge to peer underneath, she saw Taco and the kittens first.

"Oh, my sweet little Taco," she murmured, and pushed her fingers through the grating to stroke the cat's nose. "You didn't think you'd have to go through this again, did you? I promise you're going to be safe from here on. *I promise.*"

Straightening, she found Luke watching her with an in-scrutable expression. "Are you all right?" he asked.

Jorie nodded. "As long as the animals are okay, then I'm good. I didn't have any sentimental feelings about the trailer, if that's what you think. But it was all I had. I don't know what I'm going to do now."

"We'll figure that out," Luke assured her. "You still have the land, and there must be some insurance on the structure. You could start again, build whatever kind of home you want."

Jorie nodded, but didn't look at him. Luke didn't need to know that the insurance she had on the trailer was mini-mal, or that she had no savings with which to start over. She wasn't even sure she could qualify for a bank loan. She'd have no choice but to sell the land. She'd probably end up renting an apartment in town and that meant she'd also have to give up her work as a wildlife rehabber. The thought was too depressing to even contemplate.

"Hey." Luke stroked a thumb over her cheek. "Please

don't cry. You're killing me."

Jorie hadn't been aware that she was crying, and now she gave a shaky laugh and swiped at her cheeks. "Sorry. I have so much to be grateful for. I'm just a little overwhelmed."

"We have a plan for the immediate future, and we'll figure the rest out as we go along," Luke said. "The important thing is that you don't have to do this alone."

They watched as Cort, Holt and Gus began carrying the cages to the waiting trucks. Jessie and Emmaline helped. She was gratified to see that even the incubator that housed the three baby chipmunks had been saved.

"Right." Jorie took a deep breath. "The police officer said someone was taken to the hospital. A Good Samaritan, who helped rescue the animals from the trailer. Do you know who?"

She watched as Luke's lips flattened. "Yeah. Iris McGuire. Maybe you know her?"

"Iris McGuire, as in Matt McGuire's sister? I just met her this morning!" Jorie clapped a hand over her mouth. "She lives just down the road. She must have seen the flames and ran over to help!"

Luke glanced around, and drew Jorie aside where nobody could overhear their conversation. "Jorie, she was responsible for the fire. She claims it was an accident, but she's also the one who cut the locks on the enclosures."

Jorie stared at him in dismay. "What? How do you know this?"

"When I arrived, she was being treated at the scene for burns to her hands. She admitted starting the fire, but it wasn't intentional." His expression was sympathetic. "She thought she was doing a good thing, releasing the animals back into the wild. I don't think she intended any harm."

"But to burn down my home? How is that helpful?"

"Remember the cigarette butts we saw in the grass? She said she came by tonight and tossed her cigarette away near the trailer. The conditions have been so hot and dry it wouldn't take much to spark a fire. By the time she realized, the fire had spread and she couldn't put it out. The best she could do was to try and get all the animals out of the trailer before it was too late."

Jorie shook her head in puzzled. "But what was she even doing on my property? She'd already let the raccoons and foxes out of the pens. What else was she going to do?"

"Apparently she's an animal lover, and she mistakenly believed the animals shouldn't be kept in cages. She came back with some plan to destroy the enclosures so you couldn't use them again." Luke picked up the crate that housed the possum. "The important thing is that all the animals are safe. C'mon, I'll walk you back to the truck. We have a lot of work to do tonight."

Even knowing Iris McGuire had been bent on mischief, Jorie's heart went out to the girl. She couldn't believe she'd meant any harm and even though she'd inadvertently started the fire, she'd also rescued the animals. For that reason alone, Jorie couldn't hold a grudge against her.

"I'll go see her tomorrow," she said. "I hope she wasn't badly injured."

"She'll recover," Luke said, but his tone lacked any sympathy.

As they secured the crates in the back of the pickup trucks, Chief Highwater approached them. A big man, he was viewed as a local hero after a video of him corralling a herd of cattle along Main Street had gone viral. Not that Chief Highwater welcomed the attention, Jorie thought. He took his job seriously.

"I'm sorry for the loss of your home, Ms. Russell. You'll need to come down to the station and make a statement," he said. "I hear this isn't the first incident that's occurred on your property."

"Can it wait until tomorrow?" Jorie asked, indicating the crated animals. "I'd like to get them settled first."

"Of course." He nodded toward Gus and Cort before returning to his cruiser.

"Okay, listen," Luke said, pushing his helmet back. "I need to finish up here, but I'll find you when I get back to Riverrun. You gonna be all right until I get there?"

Jorie nodded. "I think so. Thank you, Luke. For everything."

He nodded and took a step back. "Sure."

"She's in good hands, son," Gus said. "We'll take care of her."

Luke nodded and turned away. Jorie watched as he jogged back toward her house, before turning her attention to helping Cort and Holt secure the cages in the bed of the truck. The ride back to Riverrun was mostly silent. Jessie sat beside her, rubbing her hand in sympathy.

"Why don't we give Jorie the foreman's cabin?" Emmaline said from the front seat. "I don't think Luke would mind moving into the bunkhouse."

"Emma—" Cort protested, but Jorie didn't give him a chance to finish.

"What? No, Emma, I couldn't do that to Luke! He's already done so much for me, and I could never turn him out of his own home! Please don't ask him to do that for me. I'll figure something out. Maybe I can volunteer to be the night staff at Honeyman's and sleep there."

"Don't be ridiculous," Emmaline said. "Luke absolutely won't mind. I'd invite you to stay at the house, but there aren't any spare bedrooms at the moment. Also, I have plenty of clothes, so tomorrow we can take a look at whatever you need. They might be a little loose on you, but I think they'll do, and we've always had the same shoe size."

"Thanks," Jorie replied. "I don't know how I'll ever repay you for your generosity."

"There is no repayment," Emmaline said. "You would do the same for me if our circumstances were reversed."

Jorie almost laughed at how ludicrous that sounded. The truth was, even before her home had burned, she'd had nothing to give anyone. She didn't even have a spare bedroom, never mind extra clothes. The irony of her current situation wasn't lost on her. For as long as she could remember, she'd loved Riverrun Ranch. She would have given anything to have lived there as a kid, to be part of the Claiborne family. But it seemed some things never changed. She was still reduced to accepting handouts. She knew she had no reason to feel bitter, but she was so tired of being the girl from the wrong side of town; the girl whose mother hadn't even cared enough about her to raise her.

"Here we are," Cort said, interrupting her dismal musings.

They had reached the ranch, and now they drove past the main house and down to the barns. Gus and Holt were there ahead of them and had opened the doors to the breeding barn. Inside, the lights were on and Jorie could see that they had started bringing the crates inside.

"I think this is going to work well for you," Cort said, looking at her in the rearview mirror. "The breeding barn is quiet and we'll make sure not to disturb your wildlife while we're working."

"Thank you," Jorie said. She climbed out of the truck and helped to bring the remaining cages into the barn. Once all the animals were inside, Jorie acknowledged that the breeding barn was indeed a perfect solution. There was a sink and a refrigerator, and plenty of storage.

"Jorie? Is Jorie Russell here?"

Jorie turned to see Barbara and two of her part-time volunteers standing in the open doors of the barn. They each carried several tote bags, and now they came inside and set the bags on the floor.

"We came as soon as we heard," Barbara said. "Miles Honeyman donated enough formula and food to last at least a week and I'm sure we can get additional donations from the community."

"What?" Jorie exclaimed in astonishment. "How did he know?"

"Word travels fast in a small town," Gus said, with a wink. "I wouldn't be surprised if you find yourself with enough supplies to last the rest of the year."

"One of the vets is going to stop by first thing in the morning and do a wellness check," Barbara added. "Well, let's get started, shall we? These cages won't clean themselves, and I'm sure there are hungry mouths to feed!"

For the next few hours, Jorie didn't have time to feel sorry for herself. Cort proved to be a capable animal handler, deftly feeding the baby squirrels while Jessie and Emmaline took inventory of the supplies and then cleaned and organized the new rehab center. Holt and Gus closed themselves inside the office to make phone calls, no doubt trying to find shelters for the animals so they could have the barn back for its intended purpose.

Finally, Barbara and the other two volunteers left for the night, and Jessie opted to catch a ride home with them.

"There's not much more we can do here," Cort said, looking around at the transformed barn. "We should probably call it a night."

"You're right," Jorie agreed. "I had no idea it was so late."

No sooner had she said the words, than Luke and Evan entered the barn. A jolt of pleasure shot through Jorie as Luke's eyes found hers, and he made his way toward her. He'd changed into a pair of faded blue jeans and a T-shirt that emphasized the planes of his chest and his sculpted biceps. Up close, she could smell the clean scent of his soap and shampoo and see the damp ends of his hair. Beard growth shadowed his jaw and Jorie's fingers itched to rub across the dark stubble.

"I would have been here sooner, but I grabbed a quick shower. How're you holding up?"

"I'm doing okay," she said, and realized it was true. She may have lost the trailer, but she hadn't lost any wildlife and, although it would take time, money and personal sacrifice, she'd already decided to rebuild. She didn't know how, but she would. "How are *you* doing?"

"Don't worry about me," he said. "I'm fine. We cordoned off your property. I'll take you over there tomorrow to see if there's anything left to salvage."

Jorie nodded, feeling an unfamiliar lump in her throat. She didn't have wonderful memories of the mobile home where she'd been raised, but it was the only real home she'd ever known. Now that it was gone, she couldn't help but feel as if she'd been cast adrift.

Again.

"Yeah, that sounds good," she murmured. "Well, it's been a long night. You should probably try to get some sleep. Morning is going to be here before we know it."

"What about you?"

"Don't worry about me. I can sleep anywhere." She wasn't about to tell him about Emmaline's suggestion that she move into his cabin. She wouldn't displace him from his home.

"Really?" A smile curved Luke's mouth. "So you're . . . what? Going to sleep in the hayloft? Hunker down on the floor next to the cages? C'mon, Jorie, you don't really think we'd let you do that, do you?"

"I'm not sure it's up to you," she said primly. "I do have some say about where I'm going to sleep."

"Come walk with me," he invited.

They said good night to Gus and Holt but, as they left the barn, Luke turned in the direction of the foreman's cabin. He glanced at Jorie. "Are you coming?"

She paused uncertainly. "That depends. Where are we going?"

"You're staying in my cabin."

Chapter Thirteen

FOR JUST A second, Luke let her process his words. He watched as her eyes widened and she struggled to respond. Was it only his imagination, or did she actually look excited about the idea?

"Not with me," he said, taking pity on her. "As much as I like that idea, I'm going to stay in the bunkhouse."

Jorie stopped walking. "Did Emmaline talk to you? Because I told her I wouldn't do that to you."

"It makes sense."

"Oh, no. I can't ask you to give up your cabin, Luke."

"You didn't ask me," he said smoothly as he continued walking. "It's my choice."

Catching up to him, she put a hand on his arm. "But why?"

"It makes sense, Jorie. You'll have your privacy at the cabin and you'll be closer to the barn."

They reached the cabin and Luke opened the door and then stepped back to allow Jorie to enter. In the main room, she paused, and Luke found himself seeing the cabin through her eyes. It was rustic but comfortable, with a fireplaced living room, and beyond that, a kitchen, a bathroom and a bedroom. It wasn't much, but Jorie was accustomed to even less. He knew if he had the choice, he'd rather have his own space than live in a house with a family that wasn't his.

"Luke, this is—"

"A little rough, I know."

Jorie turned to him, and she smiled as if he'd just given her the moon and the stars. "I was going to say *beautiful*."

Luke chuckled and rubbed the back of his neck, enjoying her pleasure. "Well, I'm not sure I'd go that far, but as long as you're happy, that's the important thing, right?"

He followed her as she walked through to the kitchen, and then poked her head into the bathroom, where the mirror still dripped with moisture from his earlier shower. She glanced at him, and he could almost read her thoughts. She was imagining him in that shower.

"That's the bedroom," he said gruffly, when she pushed open the last door.

"Right." She hastily closed the door and stepped back into the small hallway, nearly colliding with him. "Are you sure about this? Because I'm not. Maybe it would be better if I just set up a cot in the barn. I mean, all your stuff is here. I hate to be an inconvenience."

"You're not an inconvenience," he assured her. "And you're not sleeping in the fucking barn. For one thing, Holt is up at the crack of dawn and he'd wake you up too. We also have hired hands on the ranch who have access to the breeding barn, and that's all I'm going to say. You'll be safer and more comfortable in the cabin."

He watched the emotions play across her face as she considered his words: indecision, longing, and finally agreement.

"Okay, thank you." She hesitated. "But what about you? Are you going to be okay sleeping in the bunkhouse?"

He shrugged. "I'm accustomed to sleeping in close quarters. In the military, we'd sleep fifty men to a tent, with about a foot between our cots. At least in the bunkhouse I'll have a real bed."

Jorie sighed, and although he could see she wasn't completely happy with the arrangement, she nodded.

"Great, it's settled then." He couldn't deny the satisfaction he felt knowing she would be here in the cabin, sleeping in his bed. "The fridge is pretty well stocked, and the bathroom closet should contain everything you need, including a spare toothbrush."

She walked with him to the door. "Thanks again. Hopefully, I'll be out of here soon. I'll check with the insurance company tomorrow. Maybe they have a loaner trailer they can put on the property until I figure out what I'm going to do."

"There's no hurry," Luke said. He liked that Jorie was going to be at Riverrun for the near future. He'd always thought Hickory Creek Road was too remote, especially for a woman living alone. Last Stand was a safe town, but as they'd already discovered, it was easier for someone to cause mischief when there were no neighbors around to keep an eye out.

And he intended to keep a very close eye on Jorie.

JORIE WATCHED LUKE walk away before closing the door of the cabin. She tried not to feel disappointed that he hadn't kissed her good night. Not that she blamed him; the evening had been long and stressful and they were both exhausted. Besides which, she probably looked like she'd been dragged backward through a prickly pear cactus. Glancing down at herself, she groaned in dismay. She had on the blue dress she'd worn to dinner, but now it was hopelessly creased and covered in mud, dirt and who knew what else. No wonder Luke hadn't been interested!

With a sigh, she kicked off her sandals and made her way to the bathroom. She found a stash of brand-new toothbrushes in the cupboard and quickly brushed her teeth, before turning on the shower. She stripped out of her clothes, stepped beneath the steaming spray, and sighed blissfully. So maybe her home had burned to the ground, and maybe she had no clue what she was going to do next, but right now, none of that mattered. She had everything she needed. She shampooed her hair, recognizing the scent as one she associated with Luke. The soap was spicy and woodsy and she used it liberally, until there wasn't an inch of her body that didn't smell like him.

Afterward, she wrapped herself in a thick towel and belatedly realized she had neither clean clothes nor pajamas with her. In the bedroom, she hesitated for just a moment before she opened Luke's dresser. His clothing was organized and folded neatly, the way only a soldier could achieve. Jorie selected a T-shirt and a pair of his boxers. Both were much too big for her, and she had to roll the waistband of the boxers over twice so they wouldn't fall down, but they would pass for sleepwear until she had a chance to do some shopping for clothes. There was something comforting about wearing Luke's clothing, as if he was physically there, surrounding her with his warmth and strength.

Her hair was wet and tangled and after searching fruitlessly for a comb, remembered that she'd left her handbag in her car, which was parked near the main house. There was a small brush and some basic cosmetics inside. It would take less than five minutes to run up to the driveway and retrieve it, and then she could brush out her hair and braid it for the night.

Jorie slipped her feet into her sandals and left the cabin. The moon was high and, even without the lights over the barn doors, she could see clearly. The main house was dark as she approached and skirting the wraparound porch, she made her way to the car. She retrieved her purse and was just closing the door when a dark shape materialized out of the shadows.

"Jorie?"

She started violently and gave a little cry of fright, before sagging against the car in relief. "Oh, Luke, you frightened me!"

"Sorry," he said, and came closer. "What are you doing out here?"

Jorie put a self-conscious hand to her hair. "I couldn't find a comb in the cabin and if I go to bed with wet hair, I'll never get the snarls out tomorrow."

Luke smile ruefully and ran a hand over his own short

hair. "Sorry about that. I usually just use my fingers."

Jorie clutched her purse to her chest. "That's okay. I remembered I have a brush in my handbag, so I came out to get it. What are you doing up so late?"

The moonlight illuminated him, casting his face in sharp light and shadow. He held up a small duffel bag. "I went up to the house to grab a few things, and Rosa-Maria put together a bag for you including a hairbrush, a blow-dryer, and some clean clothes. I was heading to the cabin to leave them on the front porch when I saw you."

His eyes swept over her, missing nothing. Jorie was acutely conscious of how she must look in his shirt and shorts, with her hair in wild tangles around her shoulders. "That was good of her. I hope you don't mind that I borrowed some of your clothes."

His expression was inscrutable. "No, I don't mind."

Standing with him in the muted darkness felt strangely intimate, with the lightning bugs blinking in the tall grass and the sound of crickets all around them. The heat of the day had dissipated, but the air was still warm. The combination of the moonlight and the night music made Jorie think about hot kisses and long, slow sex. She had only recent experience with the first and none with the last, but she had an excellent imagination, and it seemed to kick into overdrive whenever Luke was around. After the events of the evening, she should have been tired, but instead, she felt strangely exhilarated.

"Well, I should get back," she finally said, reluctant for this unexpected encounter to end. "Would you like me to take that bag?"

"No, I'll carry it," he said. "Gives me an excuse to walk you back to the cabin."

Happiness, heady and effervescent as sparkling wine, rioted through her veins. At that moment, she couldn't have cared less about the fire or her future. She was with Luke Claiborne, the guy she'd loved for as long as she could recall, and everything was right with the world.

When they reached the cabin, Jorie paused in the open door. The interior light spilled over Luke's features and emphasized the thrust of his cheekbones and his proud nose. His dark eyes were fathomless. He watched her carefully, as if he half-expected her to bolt. Jorie acknowledged there was a part of her that wanted to. He was overwhelmingly male and big, and being near him did funny things to her insides, like the time she and Jessie had taken a ride on the Tilt-A-Whirl at the local carnival. She'd felt exhilarated and terrified and dizzy, all at the same time, and being near Luke was like that.

Reaching out with his free hand, he picked up a damp tendril of her hair. "You should wear your hair down more often," he murmured. "You looked beautiful at dinner, by the way."

Jorie gave a self-conscious laugh, but couldn't deny the bright burst of pleasure his words elicited. "Thank you, but I'm sure I look like a drowned rat right now."

"You remind me of a mermaid," he said, his voice low. "I half-expect you to dissolve into sea-foam any second."

"I'm not going anywhere," she managed to say. Afterward, she wasn't sure where she got the courage, but without conscious thought, she stepped toward him and lifted a hand to his lean cheek, feeling the roughness of his beard growth under her fingertips. He grew still, but his breath caught, which gave Jorie added confidence. "Touch me, and see."

The duffel bag he'd been carrying hit the deck with a soft thud, and then he was hauling her into his arms. Jorie barely had time to draw a breath before his mouth was on hers, and the chemistry was just as potent as she remembered. But where he'd held back before, there was no restraint in him now. Jorie let her pocketbook slide from her fingers to land beside the duffel bag, as Luke kissed her with an intensity that left her quivering and weak. She clung to him, one hand curled around his shoulder, while her other hand crept up to stroke the hard, hot muscle at the back of his neck. He made a small sound of satisfaction and one arm locked around her waist. His free hand shaped itself around the back of her head and his fingers buried themselves in her hair as his tongue sank into her mouth.

The pleasure of it was so powerful that Jorie's bones seemed to dissolve. Only the strength of his arms supporting her held her upright. The sensuous fusing of their lips and tongues sent an answering bloom of heat and moisture to her center, and beneath his T-shirt, her nipples grew tight and achy. Luke dragged his mouth from hers and nuzzled into the side of her neck, his whiskers scraping the sensitive skin beneath her ear and making her shiver. One hand slid down to her hip to cup her bottom and pull her against his body. The hard thrust of his arousal was both exciting and terrifying.

"Do you . . . do you want to come inside?" she managed to ask, a little shocked by her own temerity.

Luke pulled back just enough to look into her eyes, and his own glittered hotly. "Are you sure?"

Was she sure? Not by any stretch of her imagination, but every cell in her body quivered with eagerness for his touch. She didn't want to overthink this.

"Yes, I'm sure."

Luke released her, but caught one of her hands in his and held it as he scooped up the duffel bag and her pocketbook, and led her into the cabin. Inside, he dropped both bags onto the floor and kicked the door shut, before he tossed his cowboy hat onto a nearby chair and pulled her back into his arms. But when he kissed her again, Jorie thought there was a new quality in his touch, almost a reverence. His kiss was unhurried as he explored her mouth, while his hands moved with a slow deliberation over her body, shaping her spine and bottom until Jorie squirmed against him. His slow thoroughness only amped up her need for more.

His fingers gathered the hem of her shirt and eased it upward, and then his big hand moved warmly against the bare skin of her stomach. Jorie's breath hissed in with the shock of the contact, but when he pushed his hand higher and covered her breast, a shuddering moan escaped her. She swayed against him, unbalanced by the force of sensations washing over her. He thumbed her nipple and Jorie felt the jolt of it between her legs, where she pulsed hotly.

"Please," she whispered, "take me to bed."

The words were barely out of her mouth before Luke bent and lifted her into his arms as easily as if she weighed no more than a child. She clutched at his shoulders as he strode through the cabin to the bedroom and laid her down on the coverlet. He drew her sandals from her feet and Jorie knew a moment of uncertainty when he eased himself down beside her, but then he kissed her again and any doubts were obliterated beneath a wash of pleasure. Almost against her will, Jorie pushed her hips upward and wound her arms around his neck in an effort to get closer. Turning onto his side, Luke pulled her close until her breasts were flattened against the hard planes of his chest. He lifted her leg so that it draped over his hip, and then their mouths came together again in hot, hungry kisses. When Luke slid a hand into the back of the boxers and cupped her buttock, Jorie froze.

Luke lifted his head.

"Okay?" he asked, his voice a deep rumble. "I won't do anything you don't want. You know that, right?"

Jorie nodded and tried to speak, but his fingers were stroking over the bare skin of her bottom and exploring the crease where her buttock met her thigh. He was so close to the spot where she pulsed and ached that she could barely think straight. She desperately wanted him to touch her *there*, but was certain she would die of embarrassment if he did.

Luke murmured rough words of approval in her ear, his breath hot against her skin. He kissed her jaw and neck, and removed his hand from her boxers just long enough to tug her shirt over her head. Cool air whispered over her and she inched closer to the protective warmth of his body, partly in an effort to shield herself from his gaze.

"Let me look at you," he muttered, and turned her onto her back. When she would have covered her breasts with her hands, he laced his fingers with hers and held them over her head. In the indistinct light, his hot gaze moved over her like a physical touch. Jorie trembled, both aroused and self-conscious. She wished she had bigger breasts. She wished she had more experience so she knew how to please him.

"Jesus, you're pretty," he said, and dipped his head to kiss one erect nipple before fastening his mouth over the taut flesh.

The heat and moisture of his tongue as he tugged rhythmically sent waves of pleasure washing over her. He released her hands and she speared her fingers through his short hair, holding his head against her breast. Bright sparks of sensation raced through her and coalesced at the apex of her thighs. He released her nipple and began to trail kisses down her body, lingering on the soft curve of her stomach and the whorl of her navel. Jorie's breath caught as his hands slid into the waistband of the boxers and slowly drew them downward, pressing his mouth against her exposed skin, inch by excruciating inch. She reached for his hands to stop him, but he captured them in his own and pressed them against the bed cover.

"Let me," he insisted softly. He reared back onto his knees just long enough to pull the boxers off entirely. When she was completely nude, he sat on his heels and just looked at her for an endless moment. If Jorie had had any doubts about her own desirability, they were dispelled by the hot, hungry expression on Luke's face.

"Do you trust me?" he asked.

Jorie sucked in a trembling breath. "Of course. You wouldn't be here if I didn't. But Luke—" She broke off uncertainly. "I've never done this before."

"I know." Luke came over her, bracing himself on his hands as he kissed her again, feasting on her mouth before dipping his head to her breasts and stomach, letting his hands follow his lips. He was everywhere, kissing and stroking her heated flesh until Jorie's hands fisted in the bedclothes and she writhed beneath him. When he slid one hand between her thighs and cupped her intimately, she knew a moment of panic and her knees locked together.

"Shh," Luke murmured, shifting his position until he held her securely against his protective bulk. "Let me. You'll like it, I promise."

In the muted light, his eyes gleamed. With a mortified groan, Jorie buried her face against his chest and allowed her legs to fall open. He stroked her inner thighs, working in circles until he reached her center. One finger parted her soft flesh before he swirled the moisture he found there over the small, sensitized bud. Jorie's hips rose up, seeking more of the delicious contact. Luke complied, stroking her body in a way that had her squirming against him, all modesty forgotten beneath the onslaught of erotic pleasure. He kissed her, his tongue sinking deeply into her mouth as he eased one finger inside her. Jorie groaned against his lips, the unfamiliar intrusion eliciting sensations that caused her entire body to bow upward. He began a slow, rhythmic slide with his finger, and used the pad of his thumb to torment the small rise of flesh that ached and throbbed. Jorie pushed against his hand, trying to bring him deeper. Every muscle in her body was stretched taut, and she strained for something just beyond her reach.

"Let it go," Luke whispered against her mouth. Then he did something with his fingers that caused the pressure to break and crash over her in powerful swells, like a flash flood in a dry riverbed, violent and surging, sweeping everything away with it. Jorie was left limp and trembling in Luke's arms, and still he didn't stop until he'd wrung every last twitch and shudder from her body. She had nothing left. She was drained to the point of exhaustion.

Luke withdrew his hand and kissed her gently. "Good?"

"Mmm. Wonderful. I had no idea," she murmured. Her fingers went to the hem of his shirt, and she slid a hand beneath the fabric, her fingers skimming over the hard contours of his stomach. His muscles contracted beneath her touch. "Take this off. Let me do something for you."

But Luke took her hand and set it away from him. "Not tonight, honey. You should get some sleep."

Even as he said the words, she yawned convulsively, and a deep lethargy seeped into her body. "No," she complained as fatigue settled over her. "We aren't finished."

"For tonight, we are." He traced the shape of her brow and pushed a damp tendril of hair away from her face. "You've had a really rough day. I don't want to take advantage of you when you're feeling vulnerable."

"Luke, no," she protested, struggling to sit up. "I'm not tired. I'm fine."

"You are fine," he agreed, and rose from the bed. He pulled the blankets out from beneath her and then pulled them over her naked body, tucking them carefully around her. "But you'll be even more fine another time."

Reaching out blindly, she caught his hand. "What about you?"

"I'm fine too." He lifted her hand to his mouth and pressed a kiss into her palm. "Go to sleep, Jorie. I'll let myself out."

"Will I see you tomorrow?"

She sensed his hesitation. "I have some business I need to take care of, but I'll try to stop by later. Sweet dreams."

She listened to his footsteps recede down the hall, and then the soft click of the door as he closed it behind him. Rolling onto her stomach, she replayed in her mind what had just happened. She'd never allowed a man to get close to her before, not since that night with Mason Childress. She'd always thought that when she finally did let a man into her bed, the experience would be mutual and would bring them closer together. So why did she suddenly feel so alone?

Chapter Fourteen

I N THE END, Evan accompanied Jorie back to her property the following morning, after the fire department had given her the okay to return. But as they picked through the charred rubble, it was clear there was nothing left to salvage. The fire and the subsequent water had destroyed everything.

"What will you do?" Evan asked, as they walked back toward the road where his truck was parked.

Jorie shrugged. "I'm not sure. I spoke with the insurance company this morning and I'll receive a small settlement, but not enough to build a house. Maybe enough to secure a construction loan, or put a down payment on another mobile home." She glanced at Evan. "Either way, I won't be able to continue the wildlife rehab, at least not for now. Once the animals in the breeding barn are ready for release back into the wild, I'll pick up some extra hours at the clinic."

"Maybe you can find an alternate space for the rehab center, something you can rent. I can make inquiries, if you'd like."

Jorie gave him a grateful smile. "Thank you, I'd appreciate that." She hesitated. "Did you see Luke this morning, by any chance?"

"No, why?"

"No reason, just curious."

"Do you want me to give him a call?"

Jorie waved a dismissive hand. "No, of course not. It's fine. I'm sure I'll see him at some point today."

Evan glanced at her. "You're sure?"

She nodded. She didn't want Evan to know that she had expected Luke to bring her out to the property. She didn't want him to think she was ungrateful, and she certainly didn't want him to guess the depth of her feelings for Luke. "Actually, I have a favor to ask. I'd like to stop by the McGuire house and see Iris, if you think she's up for a visit."

Evan's expression reflected his surprise. "The woman who started the blaze? Why?"

"I'd like to thank her for rescuing the animals. I know she didn't mean to start the fire."

Evan made a scoffing sound of disbelief. "You're a better person than I am, Jorie. Sure, we can stop by there."

Less than a mile down the road from Jorie's property, the McGuire house was a tidy ranch tucked back behind some trees, with an enormous three-bay garage behind it. As they turned down the driveway, several dogs came out from behind the house and stood barking at them until a woman opened the front door.

"Ma'am," Evan said, touching the brim of his hat. "I'm Evan Claiborne, and this is Jorie Russell. Is Iris at home?"

The woman, clearly Iris's mother, drew herself up defensively. "She's in no condition to have visitors. Whatever you have to say, you can tell it to the lawyers. Iris is a good girl. What happened was an accident, and that's all I have to say."

Jorie stepped forward. "I know that, Mrs. McGuire, and I believe it was an accident. I really just wanted to see that she's okay, and to thank her for saving the animals."

Iris appeared in the doorway behind her mother. "It's okay, Momma," she said quietly. "They can come in."

Evan spoke in a low voice to Jorie. "I'm going to wait in the truck, unless you need me?"

"No, I can handle this," Jorie assured him. "I won't be long."

"Take your time. I've got some phone calls to make anyway."

Inside the house, Mrs. McGuire invited Jorie to sit in the living room. "Would you like something to drink?" The offer wasn't gracious, but Jorie pretended not to notice.

"Thank you. Some water would be great."

The older woman's eyes narrowed as if she suspected Jorie was making some kind of oblique reference to the fire, but then she stomped into the adjacent kitchen. Jorie sat down on the sofa and Iris perched on the arm of a nearby chair. Both her hands were wrapped in gauze.

"Are you okay?" Jorie asked. "How badly are you burned?"

The girl shrugged. "The doctors say I'll heal fine, with minimal scarring. I deserve worse."

"That's not true," Jorie said, leaning forward. "If it wasn't for you, those animals wouldn't have survived. You saved them."

Iris gave a bitter laugh. "If it wasn't for me, that fire would never have started in the first place. I'm sorry about that."

"What were you doing on my land?"

"I was just looking at the enclosures. I know you keep wildlife in those cages, and I wanted to do something to keep you from using them again." She drew herself up defensively. "Wild animals should be free, not locked up."

Jorie nodded in understanding. "I agree with you. But the animals in those pens were brought to me in pretty rough shape. They were malnourished, dehydrated, suffering from mange and worms and all kinds of other parasites. Some of them had been injured and needed to heal and recover. Those cages allowed them to do that in a safe environment." She paused. "Did you think I intended to keep them in there forever?"

"Some people think they can nurse a wild animal back to health, but they just end up doing more harm. Worse, they think they can domesticate a wild animal and keep it as a pet."

Jorie thought of the little opossum and acknowledged she was guilty of doing just that. "When an animal is healthy enough to survive on its own, I release it back into the wild. The only animal I am keeping is a possum who was injured and will never be able to survive in the wild. But all the other animals are returned to where they were originally found."

Iris didn't look at her, but instead studied her bandaged hands. "I'm sorry. I never meant any harm."

"I believe you." She paused. "I'm looking for a new place

to start up again. When I find somewhere suitable, I'll need volunteers to help with the animals. Would that interest you?"

Iris's head snapped up. "You would want me to work with you?"

"I'm always looking for people who care about wildlife, and who can help me with the feedings. I could show you other things too."

"Really?" Iris's eyes glinted with cautious hope. "I've always wanted to work with animals. I thought I might become a vet someday. If you really mean it, then yes! I would love that."

She reminded Jorie of herself at the same age. "Wonderful. I'll be in touch and will let you know as soon as I have something lined up."

Mrs. McGuire came to stand in the doorway of the living room, a glass of water in her hand. "Thank you, Miss Russell."

"Please, call me Jorie," she said, standing up. "That's what neighbors do for each other, right?"

Back in the pickup truck, Evan started the engine and reversed out of the driveway. "How'd it go?"

"Better than I expected. I'm just glad she's going to be okay."

"So you're not going to press charges, or sue them." He said it as a statement and not a question.

"No, of course not."

Evan snorted. "I don't get it, Jorie."

"Get what?"

"This reluctance you have to make people accountable for what they've done. To report people to the police, instead of letting them get away with shit." He gave her a meaningful look. "And I'm not just talking about Iris McGuire."

Jorie knew exactly who he referred to. She thought back to the night Evan had saved her from Mason Childress. "I just didn't see the point. Besides, you arrived in time to ensure there was no real damage done."

Evan turned his attention away from the road long enough to give her a look of utter astonishment. "Are you fucking joking? He assaulted you, Jorie. He hurt you. People go to prison for less than what he did to you."

For a moment, he sounded so much like Luke that she almost smiled. Almost. "We both know what would have happened if I'd reported the incident, Evan," she said. "The Childress money would have buried the complaint, nothing would have happened to Mason, and he would have ensured my life was a living hell. You know it's true."

Evan's hands tightened around the steering wheel. "Luke said he saw him with you the other day."

"No, he saw him *near* me. We weren't together, not even close." She gave a humorless laugh. "Trust me, I learned my lesson."

"But he hasn't," Evan said grimly.

Aside from the few minutes after Evan had rescued her from Mason, when she had begged him not to tell anyone what had happened, they had never talked about that night. Evan had been too furious to be solicitous, asking her bluntly if Mason had raped her. When she shook her head no, he'd asked if she needed to go to the hospital. Again, no. When he'd insisted on taking her to the police station, she had pleaded with him until he'd finally—reluctantly—relented. He'd bundled her into his truck and had stormed into the house to find Callie, and that had been it. Jorie had been weak with relief. He'd agreed to keep her secret and Jorie had trusted him to do that. She had almost convinced herself that he'd forgotten the incident. So why was he fixated on it now?

"It was a long time ago, and I'm fine," she said. "Please. I'd rather not talk about it."

"Fine."

She turned to look at him, suspicion prickling at her. "You didn't say anything to Luke about that night, did you?"

Evan scowled at her. "Might have."

"Evan, you promised me you wouldn't say anything." Jorie thought again of the previous night and the extra care Luke had taken with her, and wanted to groan with despair. No wonder he'd left. "I wish you hadn't. That was my story to tell."

"Luke had other ideas. So what's going on with you two, anyway?"

Jorie felt warm color wash into her face. "Why would you think something's going on?"

He slid her a tolerant look. "C'mon. I'm not blind. Anyone can see the way you two look at each other."

Embarrassed and pleased at the same time, Jorie looked down at her hands to prevent him from seeing how much his words meant to her. "I like him. A lot."

Evan grinned. "I think we all know that. I just hope

Luke knows what a lucky guy he is."

They had crossed over the Hickory Creek Bridge and were driving up Oak Street, past the school complex and park, toward city hall. Jorie leaned forward as they drove past the middle school. Despite the fact the schools were closed for summer vacation, the parking lot was nearly full, and there seemed to be a lot of activity in the park across the street.

"What's happening over there?" she asked, peering through the window. "It looks like they're setting up for a festival."

Evan shrugged. "No idea. If it's not the rodeo, I don't pay too much attention."

As they turned the corner onto Main Street, Jorie caught sight of Luke's pickup truck parked in front of the Last Stand Saloon. Frowning, she glanced at Evan but he apparently hadn't seen it, and then they were driving away from the saloon.

"Was that Luke's truck back there?" she asked, even knowing it was.

Evan glanced in the rearview mirror. "Looks like it."

"Why would he be at the saloon at this hour?"

"It's almost eleven. Bar's been open since ten. What do you think he's doing?"

Jorie looked at him in disbelief. "Drinking?"

Evan actually chuckled at her dismayed expression, but his blue eyes were sympathetic. "Kinda makes you ask yourself what could drive a man to drink so early in the day, doesn't it?"

LUKE STEPPED OUT of the saloon into the bright morning sunlight. His meeting with Slater Highwater, the bartender and part-owner of the saloon had gone well. Slater had agreed to host a tent at the fundraising festival in the park the following day, and had donated a dozen kegs of beer to the cause. All the proceeds from the festival would go toward helping Jorie's wildlife rehab center get reestablished. The festival had been Emmaline's idea, and she'd put her event-planning skills to good use. The whole family had been working on the fundraiser for several weeks, since Luke had first begun building the new enclosures. He'd told Jorie the community of Last Stand would be willing to help her out, and he hadn't been wrong. Over the last few weeks, he and Emmaline and Jessie had solicited money or goods from nearly every business in town. But as news of the fire had spread, more business owners and residents had stepped forward, wanting to help. Nobody had declined to offer some kind of assistance.

Now he checked his watch. He just had time to stop in and make his pitch to Asher Wolf, who owned both a winery and a tasting room in town, before he had to meet Evan and Emmaline for lunch. The wine and beer tents would be a great draw for the festival, combined with live music and food tents from most of the local restaurants and eateries. Several of the boutique shops would have displays, and the local PTA had donated the use of a bounce house, as well as a mini-golf attraction for the kids. Several local ranchers would offer pony rides, and someone had acquired a mechanical bull for the day. There would be raffles and contests, and plenty of opportunities to make a donation for the wildlife rehab center. All in all, the festival was shaping up to be a sizable event, given the extraordinary short notice. Luke had never been so proud to be a part of the Last Stand community.

The tasting room of the Verflucht winery was just a block down the road, so Luke opted to walk. As he neared the courthouse, he saw his father's truck heading up Oak Street. There was someone in the cab with his father, but Luke couldn't tell who it was. Then the truck turned into the parking lot behind the courthouse, and Luke could no longer see them. He stood undecided for a moment, wondering what business his father could have at the courthouse. Emmaline had tasked Gus with rounding up some of the local ranchers who, with their heavy equipment, could clear the burned debris from Jorie's property and begin preparing it for a new structure. Luke started toward the courthouse when a flash of red farther down the street caught his attention. A sports car pulled into a vacant space in front of Kolaches, the German bakery. *Mason Childress.*

As Luke strode toward the car, he forgot all about his father or speaking to Asher Wolf at the winery. Mason never saw him coming, and as much as Luke would have liked to sucker punch the bastard right there in the street, that had never been his style. So he stood and waited as Mason locked the car. But when the other man turned toward the sidewalk, Luke was right there and Mason had to do a quick, shuffling backstep to avoid colliding with him. His eyes widened when he saw Luke's expression, but he recovered quickly.

"Hey, Luke Claiborne, right? Or is it Evan? I never could keep the two of you straight, even though you look nothing alike." He peered skeptically at Luke. "Sure you're even twins?"

Luke didn't acknowledge the comment. "Mason. What brings you back to town?"

Mason gave him a look of disbelief. "Uh, I live here, dude."

"Thought you lived in Austin."

Mason shifted his weight. Luke was tall enough that the other man had to look up at him. He also blocked the access to the sidewalk so that if Mason wanted to escape, he'd have to either push Luke aside or circle around the back of his car to get to the sidewalk. Mason did neither. He simply stared up at Luke.

"Yeah, well, things didn't work out for me in Austin, so I've moved back here."

"I'm not sure things are going to work out for you here, either, *dude*."

"What are you talking about?"

Luke looked down the length of the sidewalk. People were going about their daily routines, and there were enough tourists in town this time of year to make the streets busy.

"Why don't we go for a stroll? I want to show you something."

"Why would I be interested in anything you have to show me?"

190

Luke stepped closer, until he could smell the other man's sweat that no amount of expensive cologne could disguise. He kept his voice congenial. "Because if you don't walk with me now, I'm going to kick your ass all the way down Main Street and I don't care who sees. By the time I'm finished with you, you'll be wishing you'd just walked with me, instead." He put his hands up. "Your choice."

"What the hell is your beef?" Mason hissed. "What did I ever do to you?"

"Not me, asshole. *Jorie Russell.* And don't think I didn't see you snooping around her property the other day. Let's go."

Mason swallowed visibly and his eyes darted around, as if willing someone to step in and rescue him. But no one did. Luke noticed he'd gotten soft in the past ten years, with extra flesh around his neck and chin, and a telltale bulge over his belt. "Fine," Mason finally said. "But you lay a finger on me, and I swear I'll see you rot in jail."

"Jail," mused Luke. "Interesting you should bring that up." He stepped back and indicated Mason should proceed him onto the sidewalk. "Shall we?"

Chapter Fifteen

"**W**OW," JESSIE SAID, smiling at Jorie from across their usual table at Java Time. "So your dreams have come true. You're actually sleeping in Luke's bed!"

"Shh!" Jorie gave her friend a warning look, despite the fact the café was conspicuously empty of customers for a Saturday morning. "I don't want the entire town to know! Besides, it's not as if he's in that bed with me. He insisted I take the cabin. He said it would be more private for me, and that I'd be closer to the animals."

"Uh-huh," Jessie said skeptically, but her dark eyes gleamed with amusement. "And I'm sure he had no ulterior motives for moving you into his house."

Jorie set her mug down and leaned across the table, lowering her voice. "I wanted him to stay on Thursday night after the fire, but he said he wouldn't take advantage of me when I was vulnerable."

Jessie's eyes rounded. "You wanted him to stay with you? As in overnight?" Seeing Jorie's blush, she squealed, and then lowered her voice to a fierce whisper. "Oh my God! You slept with him!"

"No! Well, sort of." Jorie waved a hand. "I mean, technically we didn't *sleep* together."

She waited as Jessie scooted her chair closer. Part of her regretted saying anything, but another part of her desperately wanted someone to confide in. She was so confused.

"Tell me everything!" Jessie insisted. "Don't leave anything out! Oh, I'm hyperventilating just thinking about it!" Reaching out, she squeezed Jorie's hand. "I *knew* he was totally into you!"

Keeping a wary eye out for eavesdroppers, Jorie described the events of the night, skimming over the most intimate details, but still telling her friend what she and Luke had done.

"And then he left," she said, looking at Jessie. "He said I needed to sleep."

"Jorie, that was a sweet, considerate thing he did!" Jessie said, propping her chin in her hand as she considered Jorie. "He put aside his own pleasure for yours. No guy would do that unless he cared about the woman."

Jorie looked hopefully at her friend. "Do you really think so?"

"Absolutely."

"Says the woman who has never had a serious relationship because she's holding out for Mr. Impossible," Jorie said wryly.

Jessie's face took on an enigmatic look. "I wouldn't call Holt impossible, just . . . stubborn. If I thought he wasn't interested, I'd move on, but . . ." Her voice trailed off.

Jorie leaned forward. "Did something happen between the two of you?"

Jessie shrugged, but a smile curved her mouth. "It was a long time ago, but it was enough to tell me he's not nearly as immune as he likes to pretend." She took a sip of her coffee. "I'm nothing if not persistent. And patient."

Jorie sighed. "I haven't seen Luke since Thursday night. He called me yesterday to say something had come up and that he would see me today, but so far I haven't heard from him."

"Well, it is barely ten thirty in the morning. The day is young." Jessie glanced at her watch. "Speaking of which, we should head over to the park for the festival."

"What festival?" Jorie asked. "I saw the activity, but the town has never done a festival in June, and I didn't see any fliers about it."

"You wouldn't have, since it was organized in secret." Jessie waggled her eyebrows meaningfully.

Jorie stared at her friend in confusion, and then dismay, as realization slowly dawned. "Are you telling me this festival is for me?"

Jessie grinned. "C'mon, let's go over and see. I told Evan and Luke I'd have you there by ten thirty."

"Oh, no," Jorie begged. "Please don't make me go. Why would the town do this? Whose idea was this, anyway?"

"I'm pretty sure Luke had the idea first, and then Emmaline began soliciting interest a couple of weeks ago. But several people had the same thought: Barbara, the Honeymans, and even Mrs. McGuire. Basically, the entire town wanted to do something to help you get back on your feet."

Jorie covered her face with her hands, overcome with

sudden emotion. For most of her life, she had felt like an outsider, uncomfortably aware of the legacy her mother had left her. She hadn't deliberately set out to prove she wasn't like her mother. Instead, she'd simply chosen to follow her heart and help those who had no voice and no advocate. Aside from the few volunteers who helped her with the wildlife, she hadn't thought anyone really cared about her efforts. The knowledge that the town would do this for her was both humbling and mortifying.

"I don't need anybody's help," she protested weakly, but even she didn't believe her words.

"Of course you don't," Jessie assured her. "But your animals do, and that's why you're going to show up, smile, and enjoy yourself."

Standing up, Jorie hugged her friend, feeling grateful tears bite at the back of her eyelids. "Thank you, Jessie."

"Of course."

Pulling away, she glanced down at herself. She wore a pretty peach sundress that Emmaline had loaned her, and she'd pulled her hair back in a neat braid. "How do I look?"

Jessie looked at her critically, and then reached for her braid. "May I?" Without waiting for a response, she pulled the braid free from the elastic and shook it out so that Jorie's hair fell around her shoulders in bright waves. "There. Much better."

As they made their way toward the park, Jorie could hear music and the sound of people laughing and enjoying themselves. Everyone they passed smiled and greeted them, and several people approached her to offer their sympathy and support.

"I had no idea anybody even knew who I was," Jorie said as an aside to Jessie.

"You work at the veterinary clinic, and those people do love their animals." Jessie smiled. "Here we are."

Someone had hung an enormous banner over the entrance to the park that read, "Rebuild the Russell Rehab Center!"

Jorie stopped and stared. "The Russell Rehab Center?" she echoed faintly.

"That's what the folks in town have always called your wildlife rehab," Jessie said. "Didn't you know?"

"No. I had no idea. I didn't even know it had a name."

"C'mon," Jessie urged, and drew her deeper into the park.

There were dozens of white tents representing various Last Stand businesses. The Wildflower Farm had a booth selling seeds, gifts, and plants. Another vendor sold honey and beeswax products. There were crafts and food items, jewelry and western gear. Bella's Salon had set up an area for facials and massages. A massive festival tent had been erected near the center of the park with a long bar offering beer and wine and other beverages. Dozens of tables had been arranged beneath the canvas for people to enjoy their food and drink in the shade, while a country band played lively music in one corner. There were pony rides and mini golf and face painting, and more activity than Jorie could even comprehend. And seemingly everywhere she turned, there was someone actively soliciting monetary donations for the rebuilding of the wildlife rehab center.

Jessie was overwhelmed by the sheer size of the festival and the amount of effort that had gone into organizing such an event on such short notice. "I can't believe the town did this," she murmured, after yet another person approached her and extended their good wishes.

Jorie paused for a moment to take it all in; the crowds, the laughter, the music, and the dozens of children running between the tents as parents chased after them. Her heart was full to bursting with emotion. Then, as she stood and watched, the crowd seemed to part and she saw Luke as if through a slow-motion lens.

Dressed in his military uniform, he stood talking with his father and brothers. She'd never seen him in uniform before. As if sensing her scrutiny, he turned his head and saw her, and she stopped breathing. He was so handsome, and even from a distance, the expression in his eyes as he looked at her made her knees go wobbly.

Slowly, he made his way toward her, stopping to shake hands with several people along the way until finally he stood directly in front of her. He wore a beret and a crisp navy-blue dress uniform with a rainbow of ribbons on the breast. His hair had been cut short in a military style, and for the first time she could recall, he was clean-shaven. The she noticed the hearing aid he wore in his left ear. He looked altogether impressive and authoritative, as if he'd just stepped out of a Hollywood casting studio.

"Hey," he said, and smiled.

"Luke, I don't know what to say. I literally have no

words. I know you were behind this and I'm overwhelmed."

"I was just one small cog in the wheel." He grinned. "The entire town did this, Jorie. There isn't a single person who didn't want to help."

Jorie nodded, not trusting herself to speak. Gus, Holt and Evan joined them, and Jorie hugged each of them in turn. "Thank you so much. You have no idea what this means to me. And you're wearing a hearing aid! I'm so happy for you."

Luke grinned. "I don't want to miss anything. I'll be wearing it from now on."

"I'm so glad." She glanced around. "Where is Emmaline?"

Evan pulled a face. "She and Cort are over by the mechanical bull, giving tips to the aspiring bull riders."

"None of whom is over twelve years old," Holt said, grinning.

Jessie indicated Luke's uniform. "What's this, Luke? Did you change your mind and reenlist? Or are you just trying to impress the ladies?" She slid a sly glance at Jorie. "Because I think it's working."

"Luke's former commander is here from Fort Bragg," said Gus, "and he's going to present Luke with the Distinguished Service Medal."

"Luke!" Jorie exclaimed, impressed and deeply proud. "Why didn't you say anything?"

Luke looked embarrassed. "Because I had no idea. My commander reached out to my father and they arranged this ceremony behind my back." He slid his father a meaningful look. "I suspect that's the reason for all the secretive phone calls and closed-door meetings, right?"

"Because we knew you wouldn't show up if we told you in advance," Gus said, chuckling. "But here we are, and what a splendid day to recognize two fine young people for their service. Yes, that goes for you, too, Jorie."

The band stopped playing and they all turned as a microphone squealed feedback through the crowd. On a raised platform at the far end of the tent stood several of Last Stand's town leaders, including the mayor. Chief Highwater and several Last Stand police officers stood to one side, and on the other side of the stage were three uniformed soldiers, standing at ease.

"Ladies and gentlemen," the mayor boomed into the microphone, and then stopped as he realized his foot was hopelessly tangled in the long electrical cord. There were several snickers in the crowd as he bent down and unsuccessfully tried to free himself. "If I could have your attention, please," he said, still bent over, and then, "Some help here, please! Could I get some help?"

The chief of police stepped forward and deftly unwound the cord, and Jorie could almost see his mental eye roll, before he stepped back.

"Thank you, Chief, and thank you all for coming out today to support one of our own," the mayor continued. "Two nights ago, a fire destroyed the home of a lifelong citizen, Ms. Jorie Russell. Many of you know Jorie from the Honeyman Veterinary Clinic. Others might know her for the work she does rescuing and rehabilitating abandoned and injured wildlife." He paused dramatically. "Still others know her for the kindness and cheer she spreads wherever she goes. She selflessly cares for the neediest creatures in our community and asks for nothing in return. Well, today is the day we come together as a community to show we care about Jorie. All proceeds from today's festival will go toward rebuilding Jorie's home and business. Jorie Russell, will you please join me on the stage?"

There was a round of applause and a few piercing whistles of approval from the crowd, and the mayor beamed in appreciation. Jorie looked helplessly at Luke.

"This is too much," she said. "I can't do this."

"Of course you can. C'mon, honey, I'll go up there with you."

Luke took her hand and tucked it into his arm, and then escorted her to the platform amidst more cheering and clapping. He handed her up the short steps, then stepped back and stood with his feet apart and hands folded behind his back. Taking a deep breath, Jorie went to stand next to the mayor.

"Jorie Russell," he said, speaking into the microphone, "you have my sincerest condolences on the tragic loss of your home and your wildlife rehabilitation center. We are pleased to have this community fundraising event, not only to assist you, but to reaffirm the values we hold dear. In saying that, one member of our community wanted to set the bar for donations." Grinning broadly, he withdrew a check from inside his suit jacket pocket and handed it to her with a theatrical flourish. "Jorie, I'd like to present you with a cashier's check in the amount of twenty thousand dollars."

There was a collective gasp of wonder from the crowd and a wave of murmurings and speculation about who the anonymous donor could be rippled through the throng. Jorie took the check and stared at it in disbelief. She looked over at Luke, who stood like a sentry by the edge of the stage. Outwardly, he didn't react, but then he let one eyelid drop in a conspiratorial wink, and Jorie saw the corner of his mouth lift in the barest hint of a smile.

"Thank you," she said to the mayor, and then to the townspeople. "Thank you so much. I am overwhelmed by the outpouring of support and caring. For many years, I felt like I didn't belong here, or that I somehow had to prove myself. But today, I can't imagine living anywhere else and I am going to prove to each of you that I am worthy of the support and trust you've shown me today. I will never forget this. Thank you."

The crowd erupted in applause and whistles, and then Luke was there, helping her down from the stage. "Nice job," he whispered in her ear.

"Who do you think donated so much money?" she asked. "It wasn't you, was it?"

"No, ma'am."

But there was something in his voice, a certain satisfaction that made Jorie look twice at him. Before she could question him, the mayor began to speak again, and this time he was joined on the stage by a dignified military officer wearing an army dress uniform.

"Ladies and gentlemen, please give a warm welcome to

Command Sergeant Major James Westwood of the 503rd Military Police Battalion. He is here today to honor one of our own hometown heroes, former Staff Sergeant Luke Claiborne." He turned to Luke and held out his hands, and the crowd erupted in more applause. "Sergeant Claiborne, would you join us?"

Surrounded by the Claiborne family, Jorie watched as Luke ascended the steps to the stage and smartly saluted his former commander. The command sergeant major began by providing a brief history of Luke's service, before going on to tell the story of how he and his military working dog had been clearing a town ahead of an infantry unit, when Luke had been forced to make a difficult choice. In the end he had saved a child, while he himself had been injured.

There was silence during the ensuing ceremony, as the medal was pinned onto the front of Luke's jacket, and then the crowd burst into applause. Luke began to leave the stage, when the command sergeant major called him back.

"The bond between a soldier and his working dog is unbreakable," the commander said. "The bond is even stronger when the soldier is also the dog's first handler, as was the case with Sergeant Claiborne and his dog, Elsa. So it's only fitting that when a military working dog retires from service that they are reunited with that soldier." He paused dramatically, and from somewhere behind the crowd came the sound of a dog's excited barking. "Would Elsa please come to the stage?"

A path cleared in the crowd to allow a soldier and a dog to make their way toward the stage. The dog wore a military vest and her ears were perked up as she walked obediently beside the soldier, but then her nose went into the air as she caught a familiar scent. Jorie watched as Luke's face crumpled with emotion and he swiped a sleeve across his eyes. Then he went down on one knee and gestured to the dog, who bolted toward him. She leapt on Luke and nearly knocked him over, her tail wagging furiously as she licked his face and whined with excitement. Luke hugged her tightly and then rubbed her face and neck, grinning widely. Only then did Jorie realize she herself was crying, while those around her clapped and cheered.

After several moments, Luke stood up. With one gesture from him, Elsa tucked herself against his leg and sat on her haunches, but stared adoringly up at Luke's face as she waited for her next order.

"While conducting operations at an undisclosed location, Elsa was injured by an explosion," said the commander. "Elsa's dedication is unmatched, and she performed one hundred and twenty outside-the-wire missions and eliminated multiple explosive and weapon caches. Elsa was awarded a Purple Heart for her injuries, which includes hearing loss." The commander smiled at Luke. "This is the part of the ceremony I like the most. Military working dog, Elsa, now pet, retired."

Jorie didn't think the crowd could be any louder, but the clapping and cheering continued as the commander presented Elsa with a bone and a retirement certificate, before saluting smartly, and then stepping forward to shake Luke's hand.

Jorie wiped her damp eyes and turned to Jessie, hugging

her friend tightly. "Did you know about this?"

"I had no idea," Jessie exclaimed.

"This was worked behind the scenes," said Gus. "The army contacted me about two months ago to let me know about Elsa's injuries and to determine if Luke might be interested in adopting her. The retirement ceremony was planned to be held at the courthouse, but obviously that changed when we organized this fundraiser, and the army agreed to do the ceremony here, instead."

"But Luke had no idea?" Jorie asked.

"I had no clue," came a voice from behind them.

They turned to see Luke holding Elsa's leash. His eyes were still damp, but his grin was infectious.

"Oh, Luke, I'm so happy for you," Jorie exclaimed. She couldn't resist reaching out to touch him.

"Come here," he said roughly, and pulled her into his arms to plant a brief, hard kiss against her mouth. "Jorie, I'd like you to meet Elsa."

Still breathless from his kiss, Jorie bent down and stroked the sides of Elsa's face. "She's beautiful, Luke."

As if in agreement, Elsa licked Jorie's face, making her laugh.

"I don't know how we managed to keep it a secret," Evan said. "Seemed someone from the army was calling the house every week, and we had to keep it all hush-hush."

"Well, I appreciate everything you did to get her back." Luke shook Evan's hand and then gave his father a hug. "I don't know what to say. I'm just so thankful for this, for everything." He looked at Jorie and smiled. "I finally feel complete."

Chapter Sixteen

T HAT EVENING, ROSA-MARIA prepared dinner for the Claiborne clan on the back terrace, and it was as magical and wonderful as Jorie remembered from her childhood. Even more so, because now Luke sat beside her with his hand curled around hers, seemingly unable to stop touching her. Jorie didn't mind. She didn't think she'd ever be able to get enough of him or his touch. He'd changed out of his uniform and back into a pair of Wranglers, paired with a plaid button-down shirt that was faded and soft from years of wear. After Rosa-Marie carried the last of the dishes to the outside table, Gus insisted she join them, pulling out an extra chair and seating her beside him.

Emmaline and Cort sat on the opposite side of the table, so the only members of the family missing were Callie and her husband, Damon, who lived in Austin. Gus pushed his chair back and stood, raising his wineglass.

"To Luke, who demonstrates bravery and integrity and remarkably good taste every day." Here he cast a wink at Jorie. "Congratulations, son. I'm glad to have you home."

"Hear! Hear!" Holt said, as they each raised their glass and drank a toast to Luke, who looked both pleased and embarrassed. Elsa lay on the floor by his chair, her tail thumping contentedly against the ground as Luke reached down and rubbed her ears.

The meal passed in a pleasant blur and after two glasses of wine, Jorie was content to sit back and let the laughter and conversation flow over and around her while she watched the sun slowly sink behind the trees, washing the landscape in hues of pink and purple. When darkness finally settled over the house, Rosa-Maria turned on the overhead string lights, which cast a romantic glow over the terrace.

"I think that's our cue," Luke said, rising to his feet. "It's been quite a day and I imagine Jorie's about done in."

He pulled her chair back to allow her to stand. "Thank you so much for everything," she said, including them all in her smile. "I've never felt so welcomed in my life."

"You are welcome," Gus said. "Very welcome, indeed. Good night, both of you."

With Luke holding her hand and Elsa padding softly beside them, they crossed the terrace and stepped down onto the grass to make their way across the lawn toward the cabin. Luke put an arm around her shoulders and drew her against his side as they walked in silence through the darkness.

"What a day," Jorie murmured, and leaned her head against Luke's shoulder.

"This has probably been the best day of my life," Luke said quietly. "I can't believe how all the pieces are just falling into place."

"For both of us," Jorie said.

They reached the cabin and Luke drew her onto the

porch where a small light burned over the door.

"This is where I leave you," he said quietly, reaching out to push a loose tendril of her hair back. "But damned if I don't want to go."

"Then don't," Jorie said, sliding her hands around his waist. "Stay with me. You know it's what I want; what I've wanted for ages now."

"I don't want you to feel pressured, or that you owe me anything."

"Well, I do owe you," she replied, smiling. "You can deny it all you want, but I still think you had something to do with that donation today of twenty thousand dollars."

"All I did was persuade a certain someone that it was in his best interest to make amends, especially since there's no statute of limitations on bringing charges against someone for sexual assault against a minor, in the state of Texas. I didn't tell him he had to donate money. That was all Mason's idea."

"Luke Claiborne," Jorie gasped. "That's blackmail." Then, on a quieter note, "How long have you known?"

"Not long. Don't hold it against Evan; I didn't give him much choice about telling me."

Jorie sighed. "Thank goodness for Evan. Otherwise, that night could have had a very different ending."

"I think I would have had to kill Childress."

"You didn't hurt him, did you?" Jorie asked, peering up at him.

"No," he said grimly. "Threatening him seemed to work just fine. He's a coward. I told him that as a former MP, I have connections in law enforcement and ways to monitor every move he makes. You can still press charges against him."

Jorie shook her head. "No, I don't want to think about him or that night ever again. From this point on, I'm only looking to the future."

"I like the sound of that," Luke murmured, pulling her close. "As long as I'm part of that future."

Jorie wanted to tell him he *was* her future, but she hadn't quite gotten used to the fact that he was hers yet. So instead, she pressed herself against the warmth of his body and tipped her head back, her gaze dropping to his mouth. "Always," she said softly. "I'm counting on you, cowboy."

With a soft groan, Luke bent his head and kissed her, a long, lingering kiss that had Jorie rising on her toes to meet him as her fingers clutched the fabric at the back of his shirt. Beneath the soft material, his skin felt hot. He wrapped his arms around her and slid one hand upward to press between her shoulder blades while the other hand slid over her hip to cup her bottom and pull her closer. The sensation of his fingers kneading her flesh aroused Jorie, and she could feel his hardness pressed against her hip, telling her he wasn't immune, either.

"Come inside," she said against his mouth, but was unprepared when he caught her behind her knees and lifted her into his arms, holding her high against his chest. Jorie looped her arms around his neck and pressed her face into the heat of his neck.

"Open the door, honey," he murmured in her ear. "I've

got my hands full."

With a bubble of nervous laughter, Jorie reached out and opened the cabin door. When they were inside and Elsa had trotted in behind them, Luke kicked the door closed and carried her through the cabin to the darkened bedroom. Muted light from the outside porch filtered in through the window. He set her down on the bed and bent to remove her sandals, frowning as he worked the tiny silver buckles. When she had kicked the sandals free, she scrambled to her knees on the mattress and caught Luke by his belt, pulling him closer.

"My turn," she said. She undid the buttons on his shirt, spreading the fabric as she went to expose his warm, tanned skin. His chest rose and fell in agitated breaths as her fingers made short work of his buckle. Amazed by her own eagerness, she managed to unfasten the button on his jeans before he covered her hands with his own.

"Easy, honey," he said, his mouth tilting into a roguish grin. "We don't have to rush. I want to take my time with you."

"Luke Claiborne," she said, her voice breathless, "I've wanted you from the time I was old enough to recognize the feeling, and I'm done waiting."

Luke stared at her for a long second, and the expression in his eyes was so hot that Jorie could feel it reaching into her, all the way to her center where she pulsed and burned.

"Yes, ma'am," he said softly, and reached for her.

This time, when he kissed her, he didn't hold back. Jorie felt the difference; the damp heat and raw urgency of his mouth on hers was like a catalyst for all the feelings she'd held bottled up inside, afraid of rejection, but even more afraid of herself and her own response. She wrapped his head in her arms, thrusting her fingers through the rough silk of his hair as she slanted her mouth against his and stroked his tongue with her own. His scalp was hot against her fingertips, his body hard and yielding all at the same time.

Jorie was so caught up in sensation that it wasn't until she felt cool air wafting against her skin that she realized Luke had unfastened her sundress. He slid one hand into the opening and skated his palm over her bare back. Jorie shivered and lowered her arms, letting him push the dress from her shoulders until she could slide her arms free. The garment fell loosely over her hips and pooled around her thighs. She wasn't wearing a bra and the heat of Luke's gaze was enough to cause her nipples to contract tightly.

Without breaking eye contact, Jorie reached for the zipper on his Wranglers, and this time, he didn't protest. He took a second to pull his boots off, and then he helped her push his jeans and boxers down until he stood naked in front of her. Slowly, Jorie let her gaze drift over him in the semi-darkness, admiring the thrust of his shoulders and the sculpted planes of his chest and stomach. He was lean and muscled and unabashedly male, and his heavy erection caused a rush of liquid heat to pool at Jorie's core.

Tentatively, she reached out and touched him.

"It's okay, honey," he said, his voice thick. "I don't bite."

He remained still as she explored him, grasping him lightly in her hand and then stroking her fingers wonderingly along the shaft and over the smooth, tight head. She wasn't completely innocent; she'd taken human biology classes in school, but knowing something was different than experiencing it firsthand.

"I think you're beautiful," she breathed.

Luke gave a strangled laugh. "I'm glad you think so."

Releasing him, Jorie eased herself onto her back and watched as Luke leaned over her with one knee on the mattress by her hip. His shoulders were wide and in the darkness, his face no more than a blur. Jorie knew a moment of uncertainty as his frame blocked out the dim light that filtered in through the nearby window. As if sensing her sudden unease, Luke reached out and switched on the small bedside lamp, dispelling the shadows.

"Tell me what you want, darlin'," he whispered, and pressed his face into the hollow at the base of her throat before he kissed his way down her front, spending a little extra time on her breasts. The stubble of whiskers on his jaw against her sensitive skin was both abrasive and erotic. He drew first one and then the other nipple into his mouth, the wet heat of his tongue teasing her until Jorie gasped and arched beneath him.

"I want—I want—" Jorie broke off as he lifted her and eased the dress from beneath her hips, pulling her panties along with it until she lay bare.

"I know what you want," Luke assured her softly and shifted until he knelt in front of her with his warm hands on her tightly pressed knees. "Open for me, honey."

Aroused and mortified at the same time, Jorie covered

her face with her hands and did as he asked. Even when she felt the gentle-rough burn of his whiskers as he pressed his mouth to her inner leg, she didn't remove her hands. But not looking only heightened her other senses, and she became acutely aware as he moved toward the spot where she desperately needed him to touch her. His mouth inched closer, until he pressed his lips intimately against her. Jorie gasped and her hands flew away from her face as she had a fleeting impulse to stop him. But the sight of his dark head between her thighs and his big hands curled around her hips arrested her movements. Then he licked her, and any thought of stopping him evaporated beneath a wash of pleasure so intense that Jorie fell back against the bed, helpless. He used his mouth and tongue to lave and torment her, swirling over the tight knot of nerve endings where pressure had begun to coalesce and build. When he pushed one finger inside her, she groaned deeply.

"Good?" he asked, briefly lifting his head.

But Jorie was incapable of answering, lost in a rising crescendo of sensation. She was on a precipice, straining for something just out of reach, her entire body arched tight in anticipation. Then she was falling, as wave after wave of release tumbled over her and she cried out with the force of it. She was vaguely aware of Luke retrieving a condom from his discarded Wranglers, and she watched with hazy pleasure as he tore open the packet and sheathed himself. Then his hands moved over her body, positioning her legs as he settled himself against her. When she felt him at her entrance, blunt and hot, she instinctively raised her knees.

"I don't want to hurt you," he said against her ear. "I'll stop if you want me to."

"I don't want you to," she assured him and slid her arms around him, her fingers digging into the hot muscles of his back.

Luke entered her in one smooth thrust. Jorie was aware of a tight, burning sensation that slowly subsided when Luke stopped moving.

"Okay?" he asked. His voice was a rough rasp in her ear.

Jorie squirmed beneath him, trying to relieve the overwhelming fullness.

"Please don't move, honey," Luke begged, his voice hoarse.

But the discomfort had mostly vanished and Jorie lifted her hips to bring him deeper. Luke gave a groan of surrender and then he began to move, a slow, sensual, in-and-out slide that had Jorie straining toward him. Luke turned his face and kissed her, tangling his tongue with hers as he drove deeper.

Jorie clung to him, meeting his thrusts as she tried to absorb the new, exciting sensations coursing through her body. But when Luke reached between them and pressed his fingers against her, she was lost to an orgasm more intense than the first. Her body clenched hard around Luke's length and with a deep groan of satisfaction, he shuddered and spilled himself inside her.

Jorie welcomed his heavy weight as he collapsed on top of her, his breathing a harsh rasp in her ear. She wound her arms around his neck and he lifted his head to kiss her, slow and tenderly.

"I love you, Jorie Russell," he said against her mouth. "I think I have since I first saw you behind that burning warehouse, ready to risk your own life for a cat."

Jorie kissed him back. "I think I've loved you forever," she admitted. "But when you saved those kittens, that sealed the deal for me. Well, that and what you just did."

Luke laughed softly and rolled onto his side, pulling her with him. He wrapped his arms around her and nestled her into the hard curve of his body. "Well, honey, if you're at all uncertain, you just let me know and I'll be happy to do it again."

"Okay," she said, smiling shyly at him. "Whenever you're ready."

Luke's eyes widened and then his mouth curved in a satisfied smile as he lowered his head to kiss her. "Yes, ma'am."

JORIE LEANED AGAINST the open doorframe of Luke's cabin and listened to the cicadas in the trees as the lightning bugs blinked on and off in the tall grass near the river. Nearby, the doors to the breeding barn were open and light spilled out, dispelling the darkness. Jorie stroked Taco's soft fur as the cat purred contentedly in her arms. At Luke's urging, she had moved the stray cat and her kittens into the cabin.

Two weeks had passed since the surprise fundraiser. The town had given enough money for Jorie to rent space in an office building on Main Street, and purchase all the necessary equipment and supplies to keep the rehab center going for a year, at least. Best of all, because of the new location, more people were stopping in and looking for ways to volunteer or help the center.

She watched as the silhouette of a man and a dog appeared in the brightly lit doorway of the barn. Then the lights went out and the big barn doors slid closed. Within minutes, Luke materialized from the shadows with Elsa at his side. They climbed the steps to the porch, and Elsa greeted Jorie with a wet kiss on her hand before padding into the cabin. Jorie set the cat down and watched as she followed Elsa indoors.

"Those two have become inseparable," she said with a smile.

"Sort of like us," Luke commented, as he pulled her into his arms. Light from the cabin washed over his features and Jorie could see the gleam in his eyes.

After that first night together, Jorie had stayed with Luke in the cabin. He spent his days working on the ranch with Elsa by his side, while Jorie continued to work at the veterinary clinic and, in her spare time, cared for the rescued wildlife at the new location in town.

"I've been doing a lot of thinking about the future," she said, tipping her head back to look at him.

Luke's arms tightened around her. "Tell me."

Sliding her arms around his neck, Jorie leaned up and pressed a soft kiss against his mouth. "Well, for starters, I'm going to keep the land on Hickory Creek Road."

"I like that idea," Luke said, sliding his hands along her

spine. "What do you have planned for it?"

Jorie pretended to consider. "I don't know. A house, probably, big enough to raise a family."

"Good thing there's plenty of room," Luke mused. "Maybe you should build a barn and turn it into a wildlife rehab center."

"That's a good idea," Jorie said, smiling into his eyes. "But I was thinking, what if I had a partner who was really, really good at working with dogs?"

"Do you know someone like that?"

"I have someone in mind," she said. "He'd make a wonderful trainer."

"I like that idea too," Luke said. "A lot. What if I were to help you build your house and barn? I have some money saved up, probably enough for both. You could rehab wildlife, and I could work with retired military dogs returning from war; help rehabilitate them back into civilian life."

Jorie's arms tightened around his neck, while her heart felt as if it might burst with the emotions churning inside her. Everything she'd ever dreamed of was finally coming true, and all because of this man.

"You could open your own dog-training business. You're so good with dogs, I can't imagine a better career choice for you." She glanced over her shoulder to where Elsa lay just inside the door, watching them. Her ears twitched as if she suspected they were talking about her, even though the vet had confirmed her hearing loss was almost complete. "Elsa could be your mascot, in a completely unofficial capacity, of course."

"Of course," Luke agreed. "Her working days are over. From now on, she gets to sleep on the sofa or the bed, or wherever the hell she wants. She can spend her days chasing a ball or rabbits, or snoozing in the sun. I just want to give her the best life I can."

"Oh, Luke," Jorie said, feeling tears threatening. "Don't you see? You already have. She's home, with you."

"All the years I spent in the army, I didn't think my future would be here in Last Stand. But now I'm home, and everything I've ever wanted is right here in front of me." He framed her face in his big hands. "I love you, Jorie Russell."

Jorie laughed, on the verge of joyful tears. "I love you, too, Luke Claiborne. So much!"

"I think we've both found our forever home."

"Take me home, cowboy," she said.

Luke lifted her effortlessly in his arms, carried her into the cabin, and closed the door.

The End

Want more? Check out Emmaline and Cort's story in *Swipe Right for a Cowboy!*

Join Tule Publishing's newsletter for more great reads and weekly deals!

If you enjoyed *Counting on the Cowboy*,
you'll love the next book in….

The Riverrun Ranch series

Book 1: *Swipe Right for a Cowboy*

Book 2: *Counting on the Cowboy*

Book 3: *How to Catch a Cowboy*
Coming June 2020!

Available now at your favorite online retailer!

More books by Karen Foley

The Glacier Creek series

Book 1: *Montana Defender*

Book 2: *Montana Firefighter*

Book 3: *Montana Protector*

Available now at your favorite online retailer!

About the Author

Karen Foley admits to being an incurable romantic. When she's not working for the Department of Defense, she loves writing sexy stories about alpha heroes and strong heroines. Karen lives in New England with her husband, two daughters, and a houseful of pets.

Thank you for reading

Counting on the Cowboy

If you enjoyed this book, you can find more from all our great authors at TulePublishing.com, or from your favorite online retailer.

TULE
PUBLISHING

Made in the USA
Monee, IL
28 July 2021